The Tales of Cupid and Psyche

The Tales of Cupid and Psyche

A.R. McHugh

The right of A.R. McHugh to be identified as the author of this
work has been asserted in accordance with the Copyright Act 1968.
ISBN: 9780648914556
This edition published in Australia in 2022 by Diving Bell, an
imprint of Diving Bell Education. www.divingbelleducation.com

Cover image: Felix Vallotton, *Wolken* (1894). Image is in the public
domain.

·

Contents

Apuleius and the Metamorphoses

Nearly 2000 years ago a north African called Apuleius wrote a comic novel about a young man who is turned into a donkey, and the adventures which befall him before the goddess Isis changes him back. In a kind of student-humour homage to Ovid, he called it *Metamorphoses* (Penguin published a translation under the title *The Golden Ass*. Unsurprisingly, it sold much better than the rather forbidding *Metamorphoses*). Apuleius' book was never as popular or as influential as Ovid's, because Ovid is Ovid and because Apuleius included a lot of unorthodox sex which is difficult to deal with in a classroom.

But one part of Apuleius' book has, justly, become far more famous than the rest. This is the fairytale of Cupid and Psyche, which later centuries tinkered with, moralized over, and finally Disneyfied into *Beauty and the Beast*. I have explored only the first half of the story because I believe it's the only part which rings true and feels coherent. The second half has always felt to me as if it was added on to palliate people who can't bear an unhappy ending.

In these stories I have applied the idea of metamorphosis to Apuleius' fairytale. At any point the story which we know so well can be changed or redirected. Apuleius' story has functioned as a kind of lightning-rod in my life, and my experiments are made in a spirit of homage. Those who feel outrage at this cavalier treatment are reminded that Apuleius himself said, 'What nobody knows about, to all intents and purposes hasn't happened.'

The Beginning

Cupid sits in his golden house, bored. He is waiting for his wife to be born in a city somewhere in the world.

Let the city be nameless. Not Athens, or Sparta, and not Corinth or Argos; it doesn't really matter which. It's big enough for the chief family to call themselves royal: a king and queen and their three teenaged princesses. And small enough for the peace to be severely disrupted when the youngest daughter turns out to be extraordinary.

She's astonishingly beautiful. I mean, ridiculously so. By the time she's ten, she's not allowed out of the house when the day is getting started because people just hang around looking at the face in which all mathematics has gone right. Things that normal people don't think about – balance, clarity, symmetry, all that – suddenly become apparent.

Her name is Psyche: the breath of life, the animating principle, the soul. Intellectuals in the little kingdom say that this is the point: although everything about Psyche seems divine, she is actually human.

In other words, her existence causes people to doubt the gods.

Her family worries about this. Extreme beauty is like an extreme talent; it colours the way you see the world. People treat you differently if they think you're closer to divine things.

Fortunately, she's the only one in the family like that. Her two older sisters are good-looking but of a different order to Psyche. They will thicken and age, like their solidly good-looking parents. But Psyche is, unfortunately, beautiful beyond words.

Simulacrum

The baby is born sickly and female. The king loves his wife and knows that there is plenty of time for healthy male children, so he comforts her with a sincere heart when the tiny thing stops breathing on her third day of life.

The queen grieves and will not stop. The king is patient for the first two seasons, but he sees that this grief is becoming part of her. She complains that her arms are always empty for the child – not for him, she says, pushing him away when he tries to fill the void between her hands. He notices that her grief has a curiously specific character, and discerns that a strange idea has possessed her. The baby, she believes, would have been perfect – a girl of matchless beauty, dazzling virtue, fit for marriage only to a god.

Understandably, her two other daughters feel slighted. At only five and six years old, the girls already doubt themselves, which the king cannot afford if they are to marry kings. He tries to console them and his wife, rule his kingdom, and stay hopeful that sons will come along eventually. In the recesses of the palace, his wife calls fretfully that her arms are emptier than Niobe's. He devises a plan and prays for the gods' forgiveness.

He sends to Cyprus, and the man comes. When he arrives, on foot and with his tools in a simple roll of oilcloth, the king is surprised. He had expected someone grander, more evidently satisfied with life. He explains his plan to Pygmalion. It will cost a fortune, but if it resolves the cold twilight of his wife's madness, it will be worth it.

As the sculptor leaves his presence, it occurs to the king that Pygmalion has been granted such a huge gift in Galatea that he has forfeited a man's natural swagger. Divine power worked in his favour this time; the next time it may not. No one, the king thinks, can feel safe after the gods have answered their prayers.

A month later it is done. A miracle of ivory, encased in wax moulded to resemble the sweet tiny features still womb-crumpled and petal-soft. The doll is swaddled and placed in a reed cradle by the queen's bed where she will find it when she wakes. Pygmalion is paid his fortune and turns to go, his oilcloth roll of tools under his arm.

He pauses. 'It won't be enough,' he says. 'Even if you were as fortunate as I have been, it's not enough. It won't grow as a real child would. You won't see it run, or learn, or marry. It will remain just as it is.'

The king decides to ignore this; the doll's purpose is to bring his wife, like Eurydice, back to the land of the living. He thanks Pygmalion, who leaves. There is a glad cry from within the house, and he knows that his wife has begun to return to him.

It is a slow process and there are points – particularly when she hands him the doll, which she has called Psyche, to hold – at which he is impatient with her. But she has returned to his bed and is, in all respects except the matter of Psyche, the woman he loved.

Such is Pygmalion's skill that the waxen covering lasts almost two years before it begins to thin at the back of the doll's head, showing the ivory beneath. When the tip of the nose becomes deformed – thanks to a clumsy servant who dropped the object – the king notices his wife begin to dim and become troubled, like a candle flame encountering a breeze.

She complains that their child is not growing, that Psyche should have uttered her first word by now; taken her first step. He is at a loss. He had hoped that her recovery would be more thorough than this. She mentions casually that she is expecting another child, and is certain that she carries a boy this time, but she persists with her devotion to the doll, Psyche.

Afraid that her madness will threaten his unborn son, he sends to Cyprus, saying only 'You were correct.' In time another simulacrum arrives, older and larger by one year. As before, it is placed by his wife's bed when she is asleep, dreaming gravid fever-dreams. When she wakes, she asks only why Psyche is not in the nursery, since she is too old to sleep in her mother's room, so soon to be filled with a brother.

The king is relieved. The boy is born; the balance of the queen's mind is restored for a while. Her illness is only known to a few trusted people who protect the matter of the doll. It continues for some years, this production of a new, older, taller, slimmer, more beautiful version of Psyche whenever the queen begins to show signs of a regression. The doll's predecessors are hidden in a secure room deep below the storage cellars.

Other sons and daughters are born. Psyche's elder sisters are married well and safely, but some clepsydra in the queen's mind keeps pace with her ivory daughter and she announces that it is time to start thinking about Psyche's marriage, since she is nearly fourteen.

Fatally, the king laughs. The queen persists.

He realizes that ignoring this insanity will not work. He loves his wife too much to show her the battered ivory children beneath the palace. He cannot ask her what similarity this battalion of dolls bears to their other children, with their squabbling, tears, games, favoured pets, and whose maturation has left the normal trail of used-up toys, tools, and tutors.

He suggests that they reveal Psyche to their own kingdom first, curious to see whether she will baulk at this. But she agrees, and immediately begins sewing a chiton for the event. Psyche, she says, will greet her people in twelve days.

When the day comes the queen is persuaded to stay indoors, although he knows that she watches from behind a screen. Psyche is carried a discreet distance from the house and placed beneath an oak tree. She is positioned as if sitting peacefully, and three of the household maids sit with her, spinning and chattering. They have been instructed to behave as if she were not there at all, and not to leave until dusk.

Watching the maids and the latest of a sequence of ivory dolls which have cost more than his elder daughters' dowries, the king sees how Pygmalion could lose his heart to these terrible simulacra, and why the sculptor lives with his head down, hoping never again to draw divine attention. The doll's chiton, woven of a fine, iridescent linen, clings to a body that trembles between sensual and simple. It draws workers returning from the fields, traders packing up stalls in the little agora, and the habitual loafers who do nothing but spread gossip.

They come closer and the maids flirt and chat, striking an even greater contrast with Psyche. When the men realize that it is a doll, they laugh, but uneasily. But who would imagine that this doll replaces a baby lost so many years before? They believe that it is a marvelous toy from the royal household, perhaps even an offering to Artemis, who guards their mountains.

Relieved, the king has the doll brought in and put to bed.

The queen returns to the topic of Psyche's marriage.

The next day a crowd has gathered to see the doll. Accepting that it has a name, they clamour for Psyche. The crowd grows over the following days and both parents realize that there is a religious fervor in the interest. The king recalls the sadness in Pygmalion's eyes and fears that he has doubled his own problems.

Eventually a deputation of priests from Cythera comes to complain that the simulacrum draws worshippers from Aphrodite's temples. With hordes of strangers behaving badly in their city, the king is anxious not to add a disgruntled deity to his problems.

Days later a summer storm thrashes their coastline, wrecking the harvest and the fishing fleet in one blow. As they sift through the sodden rubble, a message comes from the oracle at Didyma. The king decides that the doll's beauty offends Aphrodite, who demands her immediate sacrifice.

Informed of this, the queen and her women set up a copious weeping as the heat and stagnant floodwaters trigger a minor epidemic of dysentery. The king points out that plague, storm and famine are clear signs that Psyche's beauty has presented affronted heaven. At his most regal, he orders his red-eyed wife to prepare Psyche for sacrifice from the heights.

Leaving her chamber that the king realizes they have both been acting a part, and that his wife has always anticipated this. For quite how long, he cannot say. He does not believe that she has feigned madness, or maintained the entire delusion to amuse herself. Rather, it has all been some complicated working-out of profound grief, a protest at the lost possibilities latent in the dead child. The king feels as if he has stood too close to a struck gong.

In a daze he leads the procession, the cattle draped in garlands and the litter bearing the ivory doll clad in bridal saffron up the mountain path. In the presence of the priest and a screaming cross-wind, he watches his wife carry to the cliff edge the doll which has depleted his treasury and unsettled his kingdom. She throws it into the void like a tongue of rippling flame. He sees the ivory face of his doll-daughter as she turns in the air and swears she winks at him. He turns, queasy with a vertigo in his soul, into the steady arms of his wife.

Aphrodite

Sitting naked on the sun-warm rock, Aphrodite is accustomed to cooling her back with the whispered prayers from her shrines. In her temples she finds only unlit lamps, ashes and the groans of some young man disgracing himself with Praxiteles' statue.

From an uncouth backwater in the mountains she hears a racket. The prayers due to her are being offered to some girl. She feels the energy of the Aegean world pull away from her, as you do when a pretty woman walks past and the energy of the place lances away. Despite knowing that it is stupid for a goddess to be angry about this – things are made, and then act according to their natures - Aphrodite is furious.

In that mountain kingdom, Psyche is persuaded to show herself to the pilgrims who once went to Cythera. It is done tastefully; draped in a simple chiton and long himation, Psyche sits on a little raised dais beneath a rowan tree. A backcloth of spring green, woven with the hounds of Artemis and the cockle shells of Aphrodite, draws attention to her. She is flanked by two potted laurels, mostly because her sisters (who designed the scene) have a preference for symmetry, but perhaps also to protect her from the advances of roving deities.

It has been agreed with her parents that Psyche will spend only an hour, sitting still and smiling pleasantly, while the curious, the envious and the credulous file slowly past. Only a few have gone by when a woman, her cheeks sallow with weeping, clambers onto the little dais to touch Psyche's hand. In a whisper she begs forgiveness for murdering her lover's wife. Visited nightly by the wife's ghost, she is desperate to escape this curse and has come to see the goddess' incarnation. She tosses a handful of gold into Psyche's startled lap and vanishes, ashen-faced, into the crowd.

Psyche is taken home, discomfited and unhappy at the sudden glimpse of a life unlike hers, with her happy and constant parents, among other girls who talk of games and heroes, village boys and safe marriages. That night she dreams and wakes shouting, but her glassy eyes and languor only make her more beautiful. The next day the murderess has departed, announcing that she has had no more visitations from vengeful ghosts.

And so the troubles come. A tariff is quietly fixed to rent the child's ear for a moment or two and pour into it perversities from beyond childhood. It pays for stronger doors and walls for her father's house; the wooden palisade is replaced by a high stone wall. But Psyche herself has become a wooden horse, and daily is wheeled back through the well-built gates with her cargo of poison.

She hears about offences against love and the punishments Aphrodite has dealt out. She listens to stories of rape, abduction, of murder and love-longing so terrible that it leads to the eating of a lover's heart. She sees the desperate face of her petitioner only inches away from her solemnly-draped little body. Although they are adults and so automatically merit her respect, Psyche cannot fathom why they confuse her with the goddess, or why the goddess permits it.

Nightly, she begs forgiveness in advance, lest the goddess believe that Psyche, too, has fallen for her own fame. She lives in a stew of human wretchedness. She comes to think of herself as Persephone, child-queen of the damned, desperate for sunlight and a mother.

Then one morning, after another fitful night where her sleep is jostled by a thousand abhorrent deeds, she is met with shouts of derision. The crowd wants the real Psyche, the beautiful, the incarnation of Aphrodite, not the puffy-eyed teenager who isn't sleeping.

She is hastily withdrawn. Her parents admit that their youngest child looks as if she knows the secrets of the Tripoli whores and the sorrows of the Persian widows. They cannot account for this, since Psyche is more loved and revered than she has ever been, and now lives in a palace worthy of an Argive princess. She is put to bed with valerian and a pair of beeswax earplugs are prepared for her next appearance. As she falls asleep, Psyche realizes that Aphrodite remains beautiful because she listens to no prayer.

Aphrodite does not care for Psyche's suffering.

Now the goddess sits on the rock where she first came ashore, ready for the sea to take her back. In another time, she will rise purified. Aphrodite sees that her own end began at Troy, when Helen addressed her as an inferior. After rewarding Paris with Helen, that little witch had the temerity to refuse his advances. With her lugubrious hanging over Priam's lovely walls, looking longingly at the Argive camp, Helen annoyed Aphrodite senseless.

Aphrodite visited Helen in the guise of an old woman to remind her that crawling between Paris' bedsheets was the least she could do to repay the divine favour. Helen replied in a tart tone that made Aphrodite itch to slap her. The cracks in Aphrodite's authority began there, in that dark bedroom in Ilium.

Sitting on the rock, Aphrodite catches a breath of stale ashes from the sanctuary in Cythera, where her statues were once anointed with thyme honey which the bees nibbled from inside her wrists. Returning to the spumey sea, the Grave-Digger herself dies for a while. Behind her, Psyche rises, the shrines die, and modernity creeps in.

The Curse

Let that girl be gripped by a violent, a burning passion for the lowest creature, a man condemned by Fortune to lack state, wealth, even good health – a man so low that he couldn't find an equally miserable soul in the whole world.

I am Aphrodite's curse – which is to say, I'm just a story about how Aphrodite would like Psyche's world to be. A curse creates a little world of the possible. In a world where many obvious things can be denied by a trick of language, Psyche's beauty is as evident as the grass underfoot, as the chair which will be kicked in the future by a philosopher.

Into her field of vision comes a bum. A *ptokhos*, a beggar, totally destitute. Seamed with dirt, and wearing the hang-dog expression that makes even the most compassionate just want to kick him, he has a scraggly beard in which drool and food alike are trapped. A hollow, sun-burnt chest and xylophone ribs above a weak belly. He's a moocher, a cringer, whose only protection is the bewilderment that gives no satisfaction from beating him up.

And Psyche, the object of so many double-takes, finally does one herself. Invisible to everyone else, a bolt has skewered her to the ground, and a shaft of sun fallen on the bum. Psyche, the unattainable, has fallen for the beggar.

Not even in love – that anguish will come later. She has turned rabid with passion. She walks across the little agora to the bum's four square feet of grime and hopelessness and begins a display of behavior that has the crowd laughing at first. Then it occurs to some that it's unkind to laugh at a poor disgusting soul like the beggar.

As Psyche becomes more lewd, still others realize that there is something wrong. Hands are laid on her and she is taken away under guard because she is still struggling to return to him and whisper more things in his ear. The bum just sits in his patch of sun, looking confusedly at his filthy nails and trying to answer questions about what she said, what she promised, what she revealed when she parted the fine rippling silk of her gown before his cringing face.

Psyche spends days under lock and key, lying on her bed thinking boiling, relentless thoughts about the beggar in the agora and worrying her parents out of their minds. She does things they didn't even knew she knew about.

Finally they can no longer hold her. In her current state no one will marry her anyway. In desperation, they release her under her own recognizance. She goes straight back to the market and literally throws herself at him. Abashed, bewildered, long since impotent from surprise and his own wretchedness, the beggar can do nothing for her.

She doesn't care. She clings to him like a cyst, sharing his blanket beneath a stall and snarling like a dog at anyone who tries to persuade her away. Recognizing a divine hand in this, her family leave food for them both.

It goes on for months. At some point, drunk on wine and tavern advice, the bum gets up the energy and confidence to possess Psyche. The girl whose beauty drew ships across the Aegean is deflowered beneath a market barrow by a geriatric who smells of mushrooms, sour wine, and sweat. In the morning, radiant with happiness, she hangs a bloody cloth on a stick and demands that people acknowledge her as the bum's wife.

From her father's house there is a long groan of grief.

On and on it goes for years. The bum dies, Psyche mourns him. She has aged but is still more beautiful than any woman in living memory. Her parents die; her eldest sister's husband rules in their place. For fear of looking like bad relatives, and because Psyche could still bear children who might threaten their throne, they take her in. Spinning, she sits for long years in mourning clothes at her sister's hearth, her beauty flaring and guttering like a candle, spinning. Sometimes her sister wonders if she will wake one day from the curse which has taken up her whole life. She fears that day. The gods, being eternal, bless and curse offhandedly. Having no bodies, they do not experience change, so the curse which their anger feeds, lasts forever.

A mortal, having only one life...the eldest sister shivers at the thought of Psyche's rage on finding how her life has been used. She hopes that Psyche dies before she wakes.

As a curse, I don't bear the same relation to reality as a statement of fact. I carry the more limited atmosphere of a wish. I lessen with the strength of that wish, until eventually there is nothing left of me. Then that illusory world which I have invoked melts away, leaving some hapless soul on a cold hillside, half their life gone.

You want to know: to what extent am I am illusion? In the sense that I can be 'broken', am I tangible? Properly speaking, I am a binding magic. Think of me like a hobble around the fine frail leg of a horse. The illusion is this – that such a small thing as a wish can incapacitate so completely. Enspancelled, you can do nothing. I tie you to whatever misfortune the speaker desires for you, and despite my lightness, you cannot break me.

May the god's eyes pass over you. May he say nothing, wish nothing for you. May you walk unmolested and alone.

Mothers and Sons

Cupid refuses to look at Psyche. Why would he want to see a copy of his mother? When Venus kisses him and whispers, 'Do this for me,' he feels the old revulsion rising.

The corruption of her kisses sickens him. The Twelve are all bound together by chains of incest: Cronus and Rhea are siblings; their children Zeus and Hera are siblings, and married. He knows that his mother sleeps with one nephew and is married to another. It is still unclear which is his father.

He takes his weapons and shoots in a frenzy, trying to widen the circle of lovers on Earth even as it narrows and intertwines in heaven. He is desperate to get clean. He does not blame his mother for her delinquency, but he hates her nonetheless. Still tasting the strawberry and sea salt from her lips he brings his thumb down on the point of the arrow, wishing for a sharp, honest pain and the sight of blood, even if it is tainted. Then he looks at Psyche.

In reality she is nothing like his mother, and this is her attraction. Psyche is clean and pure, slender, spare, and simple. In all ways the opposite of his overblown, cloying mother and her heavy perfume of sex and need. Even as the poison from his own arrow takes hold of him, he knows that he would have loved Psyche anyway.

Psyche comes to his darkened house, where there are no lights, no mirrors. He keeps rooms full of the trinkets with which his mother has showered him. Sometimes he lies among them in the cold darkness, feeling the bump of gemstones beneath him. Then it's back to the world in a fury of arrows, causing love and chaos.

He snatches Psyche and takes her to his bed, but he is beyond all pleasure now. He forbids her to look at his face, and only visits her in darkness. Thus he makes Psyche love him. He allows her sisters to visit her; he uses his treasury to stir up their envy. He knows they will urge her to sneak a look at his face.

Finally, one night he sees her coming through the darkness with the little oil lamp. He hears her indrawn breath and feels her warmth.

She raises the lamp and at last sees his face. He opens his eyes, and she sees Cupid the beautiful, the ruined, her savior and husband, now asking her to save him.

Weeping at the thought of losing what she has only just found, Psyche takes a last look at his dissolute, exhausted face, carved with lines of self-hatred and unwanted knowledge, and lets fall the lamp. Licking the filmy curtain, the sheets, the bed itself with a hunger even greater than his mother's, the fire takes hold and as Psyche flees, Cupid is at last burned clean.

First Sight

The human face is an armoured mask of bone. Consider the size of the eyes; that's the target I have to hit. I have two grades of arrow: the softer, heavier ones scratch and bounce off. The barbed ones pierce the cornea, burrowing poison down the optic nerve and into the brain, where it burns. These arrows fly at around two hundred feet per second and I have excellent aim.

Who, then, shot me?

I'm neither pitiless nor delinquent, though I can see how people arrive at that conclusion. There's just no other way – if you explained the anguish, the indignity of love, no sane person would consent to it. People must be made lunatics to be lovers. I don't glory in the pain and chaos any more than Ares is glad of the stench of war wounds turned bad, or boy-soldiers crying for their mothers. But it's our task to body forth these forces. I'm just the delivery mechanism.

It was strange to feel what I've watched so many times before. I followed Aphrodite's pointing finger and felt something strike home, the wound on whose other side I have always stood. I have only seen one other thing like it before: when Eurydice felt the bite in her ankle and, looking down, saw the snake slithering away in the grass, and just *knew*. Even as the world darkened and Dis revealed himself, gesturing politely to the gateway which was her only path now.

There's a reason they call a blow 'glancing'. Such a little aperture, and I thought I was the only one who could hit it.

I bore up under that life-unravelling glance. If love makes men certain about the gods, I know now that it makes gods uncertain about themselves – and that's rare.

Beside me, Aphrodite was entirely unaware of what was happening. I let her kiss me and sweep off, leaving me staring at Psyche. And so I bled into that sack around the heart whence the blood drips out and leaves you weak as spring, still smiling even as you founder and fall.

Some time later, Psyche's lamp, dripping the oil of her curiosity, cauterized the wound. Nothing nips off the free flow of love faster than your lover's rampant stupidity. Now a husband and father, I look at the scar from time to time and consider how close I came. But I have never solved the mystery of who shot me.

The Oracle

I see a king coming over an empty sea. A man with an abomination in his household.

I don't see these things systematically. I'm just vaguely aware of them, like a faint smell, or the knowledge that you'll soon need to urinate. They grow and take shape, or they don't. There's no point in chasing them or asking the god for a clearer image. It doesn't work that way – though I cannot say in what way it does work.

The man packs, wretched, desperate to leave his little kingdom. He tells himself that he's a simple man. He can deal with problems of hunger, or pushy neighbouring kings. But this is too much. He knows it's not her fault. But his beautiful daughter is an offence against nature and she makes the entire place suffer. He could even deal with the suffering, he thinks, but not this sense of looming divine anger whose shape he cannot predict.

I see him refusing his wife's company on the journey. Someone, he says, needs to stay and make sure that the crowds in the market don't curdle into open revolt. He'll go to Asia and ask the oracle what to do.

Why not Cythera? His wife says.

I can see his thoughts. Aphrodite's empty temples, the garlands rotting on the floor, cold ashes on the altars and the statues staring down at him from the shadows. Aphrodite has lost her faithful to this beautiful girl. It frightens him. A father can be frightened; a king cannot afford to be.

Besides, he thinks, Aphrodite treats men as playthings, votive offerings. There's something disingenuous about asking for help because his daughter's *too* beautiful. Like a man apologizing because his wife's too good-looking, too desirable. It comes across as humble-bragging; it fools nobody.

So that's it: a beautiful daughter. The old desire of a father to keep corked up the genie he himself has summoned into being. Since I am not permitted to have children, I cannot understand the reasoning of those who summon life and then refuse to allow it to live.

He thinks that Apollo, that notorious chaser of women, might be more sympathetic.

I see the man sitting beneath a sail, watching the waters breaking on the prow, envying the tatty, sun-black sailors. Into my sense of all this creeps a wry amusement, and I can feel the god behind the pictures. I do not ask why he cares about this man or what will happen to me because of it all. I am always the last to know.

But the man speeding over the beaten bronze sea towards me shivers. Shipping lanes which should have a steady stream of vessels are empty. On their port side, though, boats from the splendid to rafts which will founder in the first gale, make for his harbor. His daughter's fame causes people to risk their necks on the capricious Aegean just to get a look at her.

He disembarks at Miletus where Thales the mathematician will be born. (I find this exciting, but my attendants don't want to hear it. Men like Thales will close this temple down. Their theories about deduction will make me obsolete. They will eventually compute the difference between answerable and unanswerable questions, and the gods will be sent packing too.)

Like this girl's father, Thales will worry about things which hold a natural and ineluctable power of attraction. Handling a lodestone from Anatolia, Thales will theorize that it has a soul because it has the power to move things. To Psyche's father this would be reassuring because it connects everyone in a system of checks and balances — there's evidence of your soul because you move me. It makes it easy to spot the soulless, or the ones with too much soul, who must be rooted out.

But Thales hasn't yet been born. So the king makes his way through the harbourside crowds and starts down the Sacred Way.

My assistants claim to be the descendants of Branchus, Apollo's son by a Milesian woman. Others say that Branchus was really the son of Smicrus of Delphi, and merely the beloved of Apollo. Privately, I wouldn't be surprised if Branchus had been both Apollo's son and his lover. We become parents because we fall in love with our own image in another person, and then we fall in love with our own image in the resulting offspring. Whether it's your son or your lover, you're really adoring yourself.

Nonetheless, the story goes that this Milesian woman, pregnant with a boy, dreamt she was pierced by a shaft of sunlight from mouth to vulva. The resulting child was the ancestor of the fat, bald, self-important hierodules who attend me.

The king is close. I feel how he has relaxed the further he gets from his home. He imagines staying here, selling fish on the beach at Miletus, never going back. On the Sacred Way, anonymous among a thousand pilgrims, the king has the peace to consider what he has never considered before. Can this story be true? Could his child be divine? Or could the gods really be threatened by a mortal with a pretty face?

I'm dying to see what this girl looks like. Why will the god not show me?

The king loves his child, but he recognizes now what his wife meant about her not being right. There's something about her existence which offends the boundary between human and divine.

The statues which line the Sacred Way, lidless and impassive, watch him come. I sit above the spring in the half-dark of the inner temple. Petitioners must stop before the laurel trees in the little forecourt and present their name and request to my attendant. They hear the sound of water from the spring and see a brief flare as the god's breath blows through me and the answer comes. They know I am here, but they cannot see me. Before my chair stands a bronze Apollo, stepping forward, with a bow in one hand and a fawn in the other. The voice appears to come from him. The single flame on his bronze face flickers like an expression.

Actually, sometimes he speaks and sometimes he doesn't. But no one leaves without an answer, even if it only amounts to: *Give up. Time will sacrifice you and all your worries. Feed yourself today and do the same tomorrow and tomorrow and tomorrow. You are not so much in the face of eternity.*

The king steps into the forecourt and I feel the god unwinding. His breath punches through me, right in the solar plexus. The attendant rushes up in alarm. My light and air narrow to a long tunnel and from the end of it my holy twin, the abased one, the whore who gasps for Apollo's tongue, fills my throat and spits out the oracle.

Forming in the god's hand is an image that stands outside time. A figure on a rock, screaming soundlessly into the whipping wind, saffron veils drenched and flying like the wings of a great red dragon. A marriage with Zephyrus? And then, between the god's thumbs, like the universe itself, I see what all the fuss is about.

The girl. The thing flying towards her, pulling light and time into him, frightening even the gods. The thing like a serpent, blind and seeking.

It comes out in a rush: 'Get her ready for a funeral marriage on a cliff. There'll be no mortal son-in-law. Just a thing wicked, cruel, wild, snaky.'

I see through multiple eyes: the attendant, watching the scream come from my throat, even as the god continues to use my tongue. The man in the laurel grove, clutching a slim tree trunk as I tell him to sacrifice his daughter to the serpent which squeezes the world. The long tail of petitioners in the courtyard, rushing towards the inner shrine, seeing in one man's disaster evidence that the god still speaks. Somewhere in the thin stratum between things and forms, a sense of divine satisfaction. But I see something beyond all this. A god burning, though whether from pain or pleasure I cannot say.

Fathers

A week after receiving the oracle Psyche's father is still shaking and fearful. He hopes, desperately, that things will not turn out quite the way the oracle has prophesied – as a king, after all, he knows that the relationship between words and the world is slippery. But still, he sits in the prow of the boat, his cloak over his head, and does not know what to tell his family.

The islands of the Icarian, then the Aegean, seas slip behind them. He gets desperate. This is surely more than a father's courage normally needs. He could deal with madness, infirmity, a bad character, sour marriages, even crimes which bring war to your door – but how does he go home and explain what the gods want of their little family?

Hello girls, I'm back. Yes, I saw the oracle. No, not good news. Psyche must…it can't be said. A father can't speak it.

You're to be married, my own little girl.

To a thing with wings.

No, not a man.

A snake. Or something snake-like.

Yes, I suppose we must call it a monster. The oracle did.

I don't know anything else about him, or it, or whatever gender flying snake-monsters are. Since everything else about this is an outrage to nature, I wouldn't be surprised if it was female.

The Twelve fear this thing.

Death fears it. Hell fears it. You are to marry it.

He puts one foot on the soaking sand of home and bursts into tears. On his knees in the shallows, with the tide going out around him and Ocean offering him passage to anywhere but this. The boatman has to help him to the beach, he's so convulsed with tears.

He spends a night with wet feet around a miserable hissing driftwood fire, willing pneumonia upon himself. With dawn comes a party of kelp-gathering women who vaguely know him as the king. He squares up to the day as they bow, and begins to trudge home.

His other daughters see him approaching their little agora, a throng of people around him, carrying his small pack, his cloak, his pilgrim's staff. They run to him shouting for their mother, who steps from the columns before their house, spindle and shears in her hand. She sees his face and drops the tools.

He tells her what the oracle said. He keeps the details of the monster to himself. If Psyche is to die, why frighten everyone?

To Psyche, they say only that the oracle has predicted a marriage. To whom, they are unsure. But her bridegroom will come for her from the Rock, a huge boulder at the top of the mountain path. It sits near the edge of a sheer cliff, like a knucklebone that some giant hand has put on a table edge. There is a thin ledge on the cliff face just beneath it, where the most daring inch out and along, looking up at the boulder above them and the clouds below.

It will take two days to prepare, and they are the worst two days of his life. They do not sleep and his wife lays out on their bed Psyche's bridal gown and saffron veil, thin as hope and embroidered with ears of wheat. He looks at the chiton and golden girdle waiting for the girl to lie down and fill them. An empty bed, an empty gown, an empty heart. This, he thinks, is what the gods give men.

Adonis

You ask: Where did Psyche's extraordinary beauty come from?

He came to the back door in rags, begging for bread and shelter. My husband was at home, or I wouldn't have received the beggar. Even though I was a mother seven times over, Greeks believe that at any time a woman may lose her mind and allow herself to be abducted, or bear a child to her brother, or murder her husband. But I could be overseen by my husband who was drinking and wrestling with friends when the stranger arrived.

He said his name was Adonis. He smelt of grass and sweat and old leather.

One of my sons had injured his leg and was running the maids off their feet. My two little girls had barking coughs and snotty noses and fevers. I listened to my husband and his friends falling over and laughing, and looked at my swollen hands, veins distended from the hot towels and cold packs, poultices, baking, weaving and brewing.

I'm not even twenty-two summers, I thought.

I had a bath drawn for the stranger, not because we honour all beggars this way, but because I was afraid he would bring more sickness. He dipped his head in the bronze tub and washed out his hair with lemon juice and old beer. He shaved his beard off and I saw that under the dirt of the road he was only just older than me. He turned to me and my heart caught in a tangle in my throat.

To be saying something I asked him where he was from.

He named a place far to the west of here, on the great mainland near Priam's city.

'But you sound like a Greek.'

He smiled. His eyes were violet. 'A foster mother raised me in the depths of —'. He mentioned the name I will not speak.

'And you have come out of there? That is rare. What did you give the Lady for your freedom?'

'My word that I would return for a third of every year.'

I sighed and nodded. No one is really free. 'What do you do when you are free of…that place?'

'I wander the upper world and enjoy the road and the mountains. I bathe in the ocean and wonder what freedom would be like. What a life without women would be like – saving your presence.'

I was not offended. I was too lost in the steam beading on his brow, his upper lip. I felt as you feel in a dream, as though you are swimming, and words are leaden things, drifting down and down around you.

'And what about your family? Are they dead, that you needed a foster mother?'

This was bad manners, but I didn't care. I took a flask of oil and anointed his shoulders so that we wouldn't have to look at each other.

'Aphrodite cursed my mother to lust after her own father.'

I paused at this. If he hadn't turned, if I had not seen that fine profile in the steam, with the gleam of a single golden flame, I might have stoppered the oil flask and withdrawn. But he did, and like Atalanta seeing the apple on the track even with the footfalls of her suitors thundering behind her, I was crippled.

'She lured her father to a cave for nine nights and there mated with him in defiance of Nature. He didn't know.'

Of course he knew, I thought. *How can you not know the scent of your own children? Or recognize their voice even in sighs? But what is there that man will not dare if there is darkness to hide it?* Saying this, though, would achieve nothing. So I merely asked what had caused Aphrodite to smite his mother that way.

'My mother refused to sacrifice to her. She said she wanted to be unmarried and unmolested all her life.'

I snorted. There's not a woman alive who hasn't wished the same. Aphrodite: she is old, beautiful, and deviant. This is why we pray for whatever she wishes us to pray for, and in our hearts know that women are women's worst enemy. Incest is just about Aphrodite's level.

'The moon passed overhead on the ninth night and her father saw her face. He chased her away at sword-point and Aphrodite, laughing at this scene among the rocks and caves, turned her into a tree.'

Of course she did.

'I was born from the bark. I fought my way through the thorns and swallowed my mother's tears as I came into the world. Even then, I couldn't escape Aphrodite. She was there in the wasteland, her sandalled foot tapping on the stony ground, watching me slither onto the soil. She picked me up and took me to…the other place, where she gave me to the Kore. And now they fight over me, my two foster mothers.'

'But you're free now.'

He ducked his head beneath the water a final time. 'I must shuttle between them, three months apiece, like a ball tossed between children. Sometimes I wish I could die.'

I saw his point. But what could I give him? My consolation was useless – with the sound of my husband thrashing about in his cups, and the maids knocking on the door wanting instructions every other minute. When you cannot give, you may as well take. That's what I decided as I eased myself onto him in the bathwater, and kicked behind me the problem of how I would explain my soaking clothes and hair, or why my breath tasted of his bittersweet perfumed spit, or why, immediately he had dried off, eaten and taken some of my husband's old clean clothes, he disappeared into the afternoon sun.

I was in such a panic at the thought of being caught that I barely waved him goodbye. But I thought about his retreating back all the months afterwards, as his child grew within me, and how he walked like a man who knew that he was just a stud horse, that he would never be among the laughing drunks with friends and homes.

When I heard that he had died in Aphrodite's arms I cried. But what could I do? Psyche was already beautiful – too beautiful to be my husband's child – and I knew that the goddess would not stand the sight of Adonis' child on the earth. So I prepared to lose her, and let the whole affair die out.

The Sacrifice

On the last day of Psyche's life there is a family argument.

She has not eaten for two days; she has a glowing headache and feels as light as a sheep's skull on the beach. She dresses herself in the room she shared with her sisters, where they have all slept since leaving the cradle. She reminds herself that they only slept there while they waited for fate to dispose them into other arms, other beds.

Someone has left a glass of wine beside her saffron veil. She smells the heavy tincture which will numb the day's terror. The desperation that she felt when her father arrived home with the oracle's message has faded. Now she is frightened in an ordinary way, and realizes that she does not believe that this body, so strong and present, will really die. More than this, she is beginning to find the fear boring and the whole messy business irksome.

No one can explain why she must do this or why the gods, who give life and its qualities, now demand that she lose it. She has always tried to carry her extreme, even frightening, beauty with modesty, a shame that acknowledges she is unworthy of it.

Standing by her childhood bed she is suddenly sick of life in the way you sicken of the false world of a play. She feels caught in lies like an ant trapped in honey.

Outside her bedroom her parents, the household servants, the priest, and her father's bodyguard, are waiting. Seeing the forlorn figure of Psyche in bridal saffron, her parents collapse in tears. There is a scuffle as her mother's women and her father's bodyguard try to raise them.

Psyche is disgusted. For the first time in her life, she swears at her parents. For nearly a minute she rains down invective on them and their cowardice, their casual summoning of children from the unknown realm before birth into this existence of noise and pain. She curses their inability to accompany that child, so lately summoned, to the other door no parent hopes to see.

'I'm the one who's about to lose my life,' she says roughly. 'All you did was give it to me – this long, unlooked-for, frightening business of days. I hope you're weeping for shame. But for your action – if reaching for another warm body in the middle of a forgotten night can be called an action – none of this would be happening. Did I ask to be? What has being brought me? And now I leave alone and at knife point...' The priest hastily covers the knife on his belt, '...because you who arrogated to yourselves the power to create, haven't the guts to look its destruction in the eye.'

She goes to her mother and levers her off the floor. 'Up! Your weary womb deserves no praise, spitting out life after life like olive pits. You want to see bravery? This is bravery – your child paying the debt I never raised.'

Astonished as cattle at the aspect of Psyche they have never seen, the crowd shuffles and stares at their feet. For a moment they are more afraid of this girl's clarity than all the anger of heaven. Reckless, emboldened, Psyche opens the door herself, and looks out at the waiting crowd. She stomps out of her parents' house, through the parting crowd, and waits for them to catch up on the mountain path.

Annoyed that his authority has been so thoroughly dismantled by the angry sacrifice herself, the priest warns her about angering the gods further. Beautiful and furious under her saffron veil Psyche rounds on him. 'Heaven has no fear of me, you catamite. Why should I put off meeting whoever they've sent, if he's destined for the destruction of the whole world?'

Sisters

It would have been easy to hate Psyche. Parents have favourites, that's the truth of it. Alcippe, our eldest sister, was closeted with my father half the time, sharing the worry and the problems which came with being the eldest: how to lie kindly; how to conceal your own panic and seem fearless; how to deserve the loyalty of men. Psyche was my mother's favourite. That left me.

In fact, I didn't envy her, even when she turned ten and it was just annoying to have her in the room when neighbouring kings came to treat for my hand. My prospective husband forgot my name after he saw her. He couldn't shut up about her when we went for a walk to get to know each other. *Was my father really her father too? Have we considered that she might be divine? How did I think the family stands in the gods' favour?*

But never, *Can I have her instead of the middle one?*

I didn't need to ask why he'd rather have me. I'm pretty enough and have – so I'm told – marvellous milk-white arms, but I look like a quince beside Psyche's split-pomegranate perfection. Although her face could have caused a war in heaven, she envied us.

Some people imagine Envy as a woman: thin-faced and green-hued, cadaverous from eating herself up with the longing for something that someone else has. Her principal characteristic is the perception of a great, gaping lack in herself. You know how it goes – you're pottering along, unconscious of yourself, just being a part of the world when you suddenly encounter something which throws a frame around it all. *Look at yourself*, a voice seems to say, *and compare. How little you have. How little you're worth.* And like the scratch that turns bad and eventually takes an arm, soon you can't bear yourself or your (usually unwitting) rival. All you want is to get away, anywhere, and make the gnawing stop. But being female, you can go nowhere, so all it causes is misery and sniping.

Other people see envy as a male quality. A man who's never done killing his wives. Who senses the imbalance in the universe and pesters

Nemesis to right it. This kind of envy isn't about wishing to *be* something but rather wishing to *have* it. Male possessiveness is boring and limited, but active.

Compared to Psyche we all felt some kind of lack. But as I said, it never became actual envy for the simple reason that Psyche loathed her life. I noticed it when she was about eleven and her beauty was beginning to hobble her, something she dragged everywhere, getting in the way. She lay in bed longer and longer every morning and cried in her sleep. My mother, who doted on her, took this as growing pains which would be solved by the triumph of marriage and motherhood. But the more she paraded Psyche before potential husbands the longer Psyche lay in bed and the more bitterly she cried.

We had visitors from Argos soon after she turned twelve. They told a story from those parts about two brothers called Kleobis and Biton, whose mother was Hera's priestess. When the sacred oxen which pull the goddess's chariot went missing the boys harnessed themselves and dragged the chariot five miles from field to temple. Their mother was so proud of them that she begged Hera to grant them the greatest gift possible. The boys were found in the morning, never to be woken again.

My father's Argive guest told this at dinner and then passed on to other topics, but I saw Psyche's eyes glisten with tears, and found her crying in the shadows afterwards. When I asked her what was wrong, she confessed that she envied the brothers, and believed that the dead were, in general, enviable.

I tried to talk her into some levity, but she insisted that a life where she could do nothing but be gazed at, a Sisyphean repetition of the same, was intolerable to her. I pitied her and although I cried until my head buzzed like a hive as we walked her to the rock, I saw the lightness of her step and I knew that Psyche didn't walk to death – she ran.

Metis

Honoured Sir,

Resolving not to give in to a jealous woman (even if she was a goddess) without a fight, I assembled the bleakest wedding procession for my daughter. A single mournful flute and two drums led the silent crowd up the mountain path and the wails of the mourners at the front were snatched away by gusts. I could feel Aphrodite's eyes on us from behind the clouds and willed myself not to look with hatred towards the sun when it appeared, scudding across the sky as if an eclipse were near.

As we reached the ledge beneath the rock where we would leave my youngest child for a husband so terrifying even the gods feared him, the wedding torches finally flickered out. Little Psyche, who had stayed silent and dry-eyed until now, gave a convulsive sob. Her nine friends, who were as sisters to her, comforted her and wept together in a huddle of wind-shredded garlands, cold sandalled feet, and plaited hair.

At a signal from me, the girls took Psyche's saffron veil and shredded it into ten pieces. They covered their own heads with the shortened veils, drawing them over their faces and tying them against the wind. Linking hands, they inched along the rock ledge in a single file of identical, faceless brides. Ten girls in white chiton and peplos, saffron bridal veils and shaking, wind-scourged arms. Even I could not tell which was my daughter.

The sun dimmed and the voices behind the rock grew indefinite. I sensed Aphrodite's confusion. The rest of the procession retired down the mountain but I hid behind another outcrop and watched the girls huddling and shaking on the ledge. They held hands for fear of being ripped away by the wind, singing now and then to deal, as soldiers do, with the cold and boredom that sacrifice really means.

After some hours, when I was afraid that their behaviour would distinguish one from another, a dark spot appeared in the centre of the sun, and a vast winged thing came flying from it. I strained to make out what it was, but it covered the light with its sheer size. Three hundred paces out from the rock, it screened the sun entirely and the world was dark.

Even at such a distance, the beat of its wings gusted the opposing rock where the girls trembled. Knowing only what I could hear, I thought the creature seemed to halt and hover in mid-air, inspecting the ten girls on the ledge and trying to discern which one was Psyche.

It was difficult to tell how long this lasted. Strangely, it was not unpleasant – there was no reek of sulphurous breath, no show of claws or teeth. Just a great darkness and the rush and draw of wind. Such, I suppose, was the kind of peace that existed before the Titans. It comes to me now and again that the creature was a kind of winnowing fan, charged with keeping a great balance, which Psyche's beauty had thrown out.

The girls cried, I could hear that much. But as the creature's scrutiny drew on, they fell silent and I could tell nothing from their side of the void. Then the sound began to withdraw, and the air warmed again as the sun glowed around the retreating creature. When I could see, I counted ten girls on the opposite ledge and shouted to them to stay where they were, and keep their veils tied tight. Aphrodite, although clearly bound to some code beyond our understanding, is an opportunist and not to be trusted.

I led the girls from the ledge and once we were on safe ground, allowed them to untie their saffron masks and dry their faces. At first I could not see Psyche. My heart raced, but looking more closely I found her, now almost indistinguishable from her friends. Fear has dimmed the extremity of her beauty and, though remarkable even to a father's partial eye, she will not trouble the heavens again.

That is my account of it, and you have our gratitude for a plan as ingenious any for which you are famed. We will welcome your son Telemachus in the summer when he comes for Psyche's hand, and look forward to visiting your court on Ithaka.

The Knife's Story

I'm the sharp point at the end of the story.

The priest sweated like a pig all the way up the mountain; me in one hand, Psyche in the other. Was he hoping she'd refuse to jump, or afraid of it? There I was again, the pointy, persuasive end of a threesome: me, the priest, and the princess.

With the priest clutching me, I admit that I sweated with eagerness. Beauty means different things to a man and a blade, but we both appreciate wholeness for the same reason – it's a pleasure to split. What I break remains separated.

Psyche had a wholeness about her which drove everyone wild. Looks are the product of light, diet, planes, angles, the eye of the beholder, time of the moon – all that. Psyche was ravishing because she exuded a greater completeness. Whatever she was, she was all of it.

The eye's a rapacious thing; it no sooner sees something but it's hungry again and starts roving around for more. Not with Psyche. She was like milk, meat, bread. You could live on the sight of her. She was sufficient. No wonder Aphrodite was pissed off. Religion only exists because nothing is ever enough.

Me, I understand that better than anyone. A blade's very purpose is to create change: two where there was one; stillness where there was movement; liquid where there was a solid; silence where there was sound. When the priest waved me at Psyche, I saw that marble skin, the saffron robe, the swelling bosom blossoming from her slender waist and I ached – as much as a knife can ache – to lodge myself in her, my natural home.

It's not malice – no more than the eagle feels malevolence towards the vole he's going to eat. I have no feelings about the personality, just a lust for the person. It's what I'm designed for, how I must feed myself; plunging into that wet, deep, pulsing well of human form. There I'm brought to bed, delivered of my ache. There, the edge is taken off me.

Frequently I'm taunted with it. They bring me out, show me the prize, and then put me away again. A sheath is just the husk, the sloughed off version of where we really want to be.

They pointed out a rough ledge at the very edge and told her to get along it or she'd have to contend with me.

She edged along the outcrop to the ledge, inching along in her red veil. It whipped around her ankles and clung to her face like a sheet of blood in the wind. Her knees gave up and she folded like a tent. I thought they might leave her alone then. At least I'd have the memory of her, a tongue of flame licking the breezes above the valley. Knives have incredibly long memories – longer and far more accurate than books, to which we're a kind of distant cousin.

But they waited a while, and I wondered if the priest wouldn't crawl out there to the ledge and bring us all together after all. In the dying light I began to perk up.

But then she did it. Without warning, she bolted for the edge like a sprinter, casting off her flame-red bridal veil as she went over. And I'm telling you, she flew, for a moment. The wind caught her, spread out those silken robes like a dragon clothed in the sun, and carried her a little way, before she plunged sharply and vanished from view.

Her scream was a terrible tease to me, clutched tight in the priest's grimy hand. I could have brought her to that. I could.

Afterlife I

There is a brief moment when Psyche's legs patter on air beneath her feet. She crashes to earth. Everything shatters like eggshell; the femur is driven into the pelvis, pushing the organs up and up. At some microscopic point, Psyche's heart really is in her mouth. There is a fifth of a second between her eyes seeing the ground and her brain realizing what she is seeing.

That astonishing unity of form which has caused so much trouble is atomized.

Inside the impact crater Psyche turns to face downwards. She begins to move inward, the ground giving way as she pushes on. It feels like a dry film of earth and something else, neither heavy nor resistant, and almost pleasant to push against. It is the fluid illusion of a self, composed of memories from her life, now leaving her autolysing cells like doves released from a columbarium. Individual memories are zipping past her consciousness, which slides into the earth as it disbands itself.

Finally there is nothing else to push against. She is in a meadow full of tall gray-white flowers, bordered on one side by a line of poplars that stretch off into a hazy distance, and on the other by a river. There is no sun, just a dull ambient light which passes over the fields in bands, like a searchlight or a great hand brushing up and down the nap of velvet. As the bands of light wander over the pale flowers, discrete shadows appear and disappear, figures standing among the tall stalks, as Psyche also stands.

She sits down, and the tall pale spears close around her. This is the afterlife of the common person. Reaching into her fast-fading memory she remembers the wicked thing promised by the oracle. This is it: not a person or a creature, but a state of being. An anodyne eternity surrounded by the utterly average. Peeping above her asphodel parapet she can see other walkers in the fields more clearly. They stand, staring into a distance which is just more of the same.

Witless, without desire, without pleasure, without sense of time, just as they have lived.

The flowers part as something moves through them. She feels the warm breath of horses on her neck. A black chariot materializes from the glow, black horses driven by Hades, who removes his helmet of invisibility.

Before her eyes, aspects of Hades play. He shivers from a middle-aged man with a creased brow and lonely eyes, to a youth burning with desire and traces of the abyss from which he sprang. He introduces himself and explains that he is alone for half of every year and offers her the vacant throne of his wife while she returns to her mother.

The alternative is a drink from the river Lethe and an eternity in the Asphodel Meadows. Amnesiac, inert, invisible, reduced to the most basic state of being.

He draws her to the riverbank and dips his helmet in the water. 'Drink and forget, or take my hand and reign.'

Psyche looks at the water oscillating in his helmet and imagines the half-year beside him. More sitting still and being stared at. A husband – half a husband – who loves her face and knows nothing about her.

She takes his helmet and drains it to the last drop.

Afterlife II

Looking into his shield, Perseus realizes with a shock that Medusa is his twin. Perhaps it is this that makes him press on and deliver the killing stroke. With this blow Perseus frees both Medusa and Andromeda from the pain caused by parents.

Pegasus, also born into servitude, feels Perseus' knee press into his side. They swoop downwards towards the rock where Andromeda is chained. A furious sea lashes her and she sees only the winged horse coming out of the sun – Perseus is wearing Hades' helmet of invisibility, which he had put on before cutting off Medusa's head. He did this out of vanity, in case the gorgon's gaze turned him to stone – he did not want to be seen like that for eternity, so he put on the helmet and vanished.

Now, holding Pegasus' mane with one hand, and fumbling in the knapsack with another, Perseus feels for Medusa's head. The snakes still writhe and bite, and the whole thing drips a gelid gore which has soaked through the bag, smearing his thigh. He pulls it out and brandishes it as Cetus comes thrashing out of the ocean, his huge mouth reaching for Andromeda.

Pegasus turns to see the face, still snapping and writhing in death. Unbalanced, Perseus loses his seat and tumbles from the horse's back.

He falls facing upwards, Pegasus' wings beating above him, and Andromeda screaming below. From behind a cloud a vast brightness peeps out and he knows that his father Zeus is watching. Even as he falls, Perseus still fears looking. He gives a long yell as the sea shears up to meet him, grey and smashing.

I woke, shouting. My wife stood beside me on a riverbank. She had the colourless look of the dead, and the tang of their grim acceptance hung around her.

'You killed me,' I said, feeling foolish. 'Why?'

She ignored the question. 'Did you dream of Perseus?'

'I did. I fell from Pegasus with the gorgon's head in my hand. I was falling and falling, and then I woke up.'

'I dreamed the same thing. I woke up and everything was clear. Clearer than it had been for years.'

I asked, 'Will some Perseus save Psyche?'

At the sound of our daughter's name, she turned bland eyes to me. 'You fool – can't you see that Perseus is death? We have chained Psyche and all our children to the rock. The rock is Thought, to which we chain them at birth, and there they are consumed by Life, the monster which knows only its own appetite. Death alone can save her.'

I noticed that she still carried the knife with which she had sent me here. 'Is Psyche dead?'

She raised the blade and looked at it. 'And the other two. Now I can't put this down. I suppose it's fair.'

There was no point in getting angry. The deed was done and the air of the place dampened fury. 'Where are the girls now?'

She spread her hands, the knife still stuck to her palm. 'Since they hadn't done anything wrong, I expect they've gone somewhere else.'

I looked at the river, which flowed grey and stone-smooth before us. Stands of black reeds like a garden of swords stood between the water and the bank. 'We could have lived and expiated what we've done,' I said. 'We can do nothing here.'

'That's the point,' she said. 'We would have waited a while and then had more children, in memory of the one we'd lost, or because the gods had fallen silent, or because the scale of our crime slipped our minds. There's always an excuse. Here, we can't do anything, nor can we forget.' She gestured to the river. 'Try to drink.'

I knelt down and stirred the water with my hand. It reflected nothing. I cupped my hands and brought some to my mouth, but it trickled away. I bent to the surface itself but I couldn't fetch up so much as a splash to drink.

I sat back on my heels. Lethe was denied to us. We would wander forever on this side of the river, full of remorse for the rashness which seemed to be our nature. 'I didn't choose this. I haven't murdered my daughters.'

She gave a joyless laugh. 'We are together for eternity, with the power to bind and loose, the memory of our children, and the knowledge that we have placed them beyond suffering. Isn't this how we define heaven?'

Zephyr

I am the first force of which Psyche was aware when she jumped. Her astonishing beauty struck everyone else; I am what struck her. It was never Psyche's beauty which captured me, but her candor. Her fearlessness in despair, the grace with which she gave herself up to me.

I am Velocity. A Zephyr. Transposer of falling women; bringer of benediction to the suicides; patron of the arena where men become gods. I am the nexus of direction and matter.

I tell you, at sixteen Psyche had a greater heart than Diomedes, killer of men. Casting one look behind her at the rabble, she shed not a single tear. Being inhuman, I am not interested in their embodied clumsiness, but Cupid instructed me to wait for her, so I hung there in the thermals for a little, watching the whole scene.

I am not so easily commanded. I'd bring her, I said, if she steps into my hands. I am merely speed. I have authority over them once they give themselves up to me. If she won't, she can stay on that rock and rot; you'll have to find another way. My Lord.

But he only smiled and assured me that she would. There is no bad blood between us; many have sought me without his help, and I'm perfectly happy contemplating myself in the katabatic winds. Mankind loves speed, but people break so easily that it's unwise to become attached to them.

It's gratifying, though, that I didn't grab her. I am a natural force of a higher kind; it's demeaning to snatch a body the way the gods do. Zeus, Poseidon, Apollo, all those sticky-fingered rapists with their clumsy abductions.

I saw her place one hand over her chest, summoning the courage that held her atoms together, and step off into the nothing. Or rather, into me. She hung there for a fragment for a second. I have abstracted that fragment from time and kept it. It only exists in a way which makes sense to me. I watch it now and again, to have a little of her, when the silkiness of acceleration isn't enough to amuse me.

I removed her from a world of men to one of gods. I transposed her to a state where the very laws of physics were still freshly steaming from the anvil and the slack tub.

She hung for a second, then crossed into my arms. She knew instinctively how to make the most of me, to bring me to my greatest force. She spread her arms, widening herself against me, taking as much of me as she could. We shuddered pleasurably at the exquisite drag. She remained conscious all the way down where I halted with her just above the ground. Regrettably, the ground is not a natural bed for me, and so I left her there and in the meters per second per second in which I am found, I think of her.

Landing

Exhausted by the terror of her jump from the cliff, Psyche is unconscious before the Zephyr lays her down in the grove. Now she sleeps like a harvest mouse in a twist of sweet grass.

The sleep of heroes is only interesting if it has some ulterior purpose, like allowing a god to visit their dreams, or for nefarious action to happen nearby, or a lover to mistake this sleep for death. So we do not know how long Psyche sleeps, or what creatures watch over her, or who covers her with a blanket of meadowsweet, just that when she wakes it is only her need to pee that convinces her she is not dead, because the dead have no bladders.

As she hops from behind the tree she has used to answer a need more pressing than love or death, she sees that she has landed in a sacred grove. Trees have been cleared to let in the light so that gods and timid farmers can transact sacrifice. She feels a divine presence but cannot put her finger on it. It is a kind of heavy pressure, like the beginning of a headache, or a thunderstorm. Everything around her has the weird smoothness of dreams and, like an iron filing before a magnet, she is drawn somewhere else.

She walks away from the curl of grass where she slept. Looking back she sees that it has already sprung up again. She is aware of her filthy gown, black nails, the tangle of hair in which leaves and wilted flowers from her bridal chaplet are still woven.

She stops before the marble steps of a vast, silent house and takes in the citronwood roof, the ivory reliefs beneath shining columns, the floors inlaid with winking mosaics. They show deer, horses, boar and bison, mice, birds, lions winged and unwinged. All in pairs, or with young. All facing front and only a little less than lifesize. She stands still in the portico, trying to put her finger on what troubles her.

It is not the display of wealth which. It is the stillness, the lack of any living thing and the copies, images of things, everywhere. It is intended to please, perhaps even to awe, but it seems controlling and lonely. This is the power into whose realm she has fallen.

Detour

Psyche tracks mercilessly. My mother has nothing on her for sheer tenacity. I am barricaded into my own treasury with only my arm to hold shut the door. Whimpering - me, the god whom even Zeus fears.

It wasn't supposed to be like this. I saw the pale, creamy skin, the dark hair, the bright eyes and youth which I foolishly read as fragility, the kind of untutored, malleable character that will never pose a challenge. A vessel which would contain – perhaps even respond a little - to my desire.

There were signs, but when you're dazzled you never see them. I should have noticed how hard she took it when no one came to propose marriage. Her parents, whose bovine placidity I assumed would be in her blood too, displayed her like a bowl of apples. What she wanted was the teeth, the tearing, the desperation of love.

It should have given me pause when she told them to bring it on. To produce this terrifying husband that the Oracle foretold, even if he brought the destruction of the whole world. Or when she stepped off the edge of the cliff, spread wide her arms, and flung herself at the startled Zephyr like a great saffron dragon.

I was too busy here, getting things ready. I wanted to take time, do it properly. I wanted us to last. I wanted nothing like my father's or my brothers' hasty abductions, impregnating girls and then slinking off. I wanted to know what the long slow draw of mortal marriage felt like, and why they all keep doing it. So I prepared a marriage bed, with the pastos and garlands, long windows open to the river and the moon, and the garden beyond. I told the servants to draw a bath and get food and fresh clothes ready. And then I waited.

Eventually the Zephyr came and told me, with many apologies and trembling, that Psyche had gone the other way.

'What do you mean, the other way?'

'I put her in the clearing, as you instructed, and let her sleep off the shock. When she woke, though, she didn't head towards the house, but into the forest, where I lost her.'

So there we were, a god and a gust of wind, sitting beside a cooling bath and curling sweetmeats, with no girl. I waited until well after midnight, and went to bed, assuming she would come, hungry and tired, after a night in the open.

But Psyche stayed in the forests. After some weeks it was clear that she had no intention of seeking out the comforts of my palace. I looked for her but my divine gaze only goes so far. Where there is no human desire, I cannot see. Psyche stayed in the forests and the mountains, and I caught glimpses of her only when she broke cover and came into a clearing, or when human hunters spied her high in the cliffs. She had lost none of her beauty, but the wild had put a fine, keen edge on her, sharpening her to something elemental.

I should have feared.

She was out there for many months: at first in the remains of her bridal gown, torn short as a huntress' chiton, the veil used to bandage her cuts and grazes. Then when the snow fell, in furs, holding a flint-tipped spear. I realized she had learned how to kill. I went to Artemis and complained. At the mention of Psyche's name, my huntress-niece paused and said that Psyche was not a member of her sworn band of virgins, and so she had no authority over the girl. I pressed her, and she said that Psyche was something older and more terrifying. Thinking that my niece was a foolish spinster, I gave up.

Eventually, though, Psyche came.

The first I knew was a ripple of unease among the servants, and then the faint smell of wind and speed, of the night falling among the pine trees and the last heat of the day leaching out of the cliffs. A predator was in my halls. The wild had come home.

For the first time, I feared. Not the anxiety which causes mortals to turn to us, but the panic that runs through a herd and leads to a stampede. I fled the marital chamber I had prepared, tore down the corridors, now dark because she had extinguished the torches the better to hunt me. I heard her footsteps, light and relentless, and I caught myself whimpering. I barricaded myself into treasuries which had never been locked. I tried not to weep at my own stupidity. Now Psyche knows how it feels to be divine.

She kept me there all night, making just enough noise to let me know that she was roaming; fur-clad, flint-knived, hungry. There was an unspeakable, terrified squeaking just before dawn and when I peeped out there was a pool of blood and entrails before the threshold, like the mockery of an offering.

She must sleep during the day, but not in my bed. I expect she goes back to some den in the forest, leaving me to clear up the blood from her nocturnal hunting, and to wean myself a little more off her savage, spectacular face. I thought about going to Olympus and presenting them with my predicament, demanding that Hephaestus make me some snare like the one he used to trap my mother and her lover. But I fear being laughed at. Desire himself, trapped like a rat in his own halls, stalked by a teenage girl who prefers the embrace of the wilderness to him. It is ridiculous.

Maybe she'll tire of it. But even if she let me out, I'd be impotent with shame and fear. I'll have to stay here among this useless treasure and keep very

very

quiet.

The House of Desire

Make no mistake: Psyche entered of her own free will. Desire is a house – you enter it. It doesn't abduct you.

It's true; I *do* have beautiful things. My silver walls, my inlaid floors, my treasure caches. But those are out front, near the door. The real business goes on in the backrooms. My empty, stone-floored chambers, windowless and freezing, where single souls howl at their private moons.

Every room has a door and anyone can leave at any time. Providing they can still see. And move.

Actually, that's not strictly true: some rooms have no external door. Freedom is harmful to my longer-term residents. They like the tight, fiercely-hot spaces in which there is only room for their breath, their craving, and nothing more.

I contain multitudes of which Psyche will never be aware.

She hears them when she comes in, but she doesn't recognize the sighs, which I find ironic in a girl named for the breath of life. Reciprocity is only a few letters removed from respiration; but in the difference lies madness.

Psyche knows nothing about this. She stands very still in the dark cool hall and tries to place the feeling. It's not a full-blown cry from her viscera, like the lamb instinctively fleeing the wolf. It's just a tingle at the back of her nose. Just when it threatens to turn her to jelly, it passes.

I'm impressed. Most people come plunging through the front door and barrel around inside like a fox tied to a burning brand. They orbit the house like maddened satellites, doing the same burst-and-run-through over and over until they fall aside. The garden's full of them.

Most people will tell you I am a prison. I acknowledge that many residents find things uncomfortable at times. But as I said, providing you still have thumbs, you can turn the handle and leave any time.

I even have testimonials.

Some years from now, in the middle of a dinner party, Socrates will admit that desire helps the soul remember beauty in its purest form. The sudden burning leads to a memory of the Good, if you stay on the (dusty, boring, self-satisfied) track of wisdom. He'll advertise my spaces as a kind of gymnasium where you can move up the weight grades: from desiring the flesh, to desiring your lover's goodness, to desiring the Good. Needless to say, Socrates has never been game to step over my threshold; he's hovered around it a few times, but he lacks the courage to step forward. He's a kind of homunculus, in my opinion. He doesn't really possess human drives. He's just a very good simulation. Follow your god, Socrates, and we'll see where you end up.

Look into my very furthest recesses and you'll see snuffling things which were once people running on four legs and baying for a mate. This atavism horrifies folk like Socrates, but it is a kind of apotheosis. Humans are a rational animal – desire can make us divine by promoting the rational side or the animal side. I've housed several divine beasts, and not a few beastly gods. The desire of a dog to love is more divine, surely, than the desire of a god to punish.

Psyche will think about this as she lies in my darkened chambers, feeling unwhole, wondering what will fill this gap. At the moment, however, she is only glad of the gentle breezes which run through the house. Until one of the breaths of air touches her shoulder and speaks.

Servants in the House of Desire

Crossing the threshold, Psyche looks into the first room and sees a glint of gold, the twinkle of jewels strewn about. She is old enough to feel embarrassed by this careless, tasteless display of wealth, but not so old that she ignores the message. *Only precious things come into this house.* A woman would conclude that this is a slightly awkward compliment from a man with more money than knowledge of good people. But she is not a woman. Not yet.

She turns away, conscious of being tired, footsore, hungry, and dirty. A golden laver and basin are all very well, but she'd rather have them full of hot soapy water.

'It's all yours, you know,' a female voice at her ear says.

Psyche gives an unmaidenly yell of fright. The voice answers with a little laugh.

'Sorry. I just wanted to see what you'd do.'

There is no one there. Psyche wishes she had the knack of fainting at will. There is a waiting silence. All at once, she decides to give up and let the world be as strange as it is, without asking why, or what next. In the cool air of the corridor she feels the voice watching her moment of decision.

'This is your home. We—', other female voices in the hallway greet her, '—are your tiring women. Come and rest a while. Have a bath and eat.' A cool hand, invisible but feminine, lands on her shoulder. She is led away to other rooms, catching dim glimpses of this house which is now her home.

Their invisible touch undresses her and hands her into a bath. Their indrawn breath makes her blush. They praise her flame-shaped waist, her calves, her shoulders. Their tears, falling from unseen eyes, suggest that they are not entirely glad to be rid of their visible selves, shucked like oysters from the whirligig of living flesh.

And when she has eaten and her stomach looks like an unopened tulip under her fine peplos, they sing for her. It is part of Cupid's magic that she does not understand what they sing, or hear the longing in their voices.

Hail, they tell her, *greatly favoured among women.*
You will come to know that force on which the world turns.
He emerged, parentless, from Darkness,
Only then did everything fall into the way of sexual union.
Natural to him is the crashing together of elements
Like a baby playing with stones.
What would happen if he stopped?
Atoms call to atoms;
Matter wants to be made;
Once made, it wants to recombine.
Hail, mistress of that tiny, white-hot space
In which the universe is made, endlessly.

And so they bless her, and take her through the dark corridors of Cupid's golden palace, and lay her in his bed. She tries to imagine what would have happened if she had refused to go, or made a break for the door. Sleep overcomes her but as she drifts off she sees someone standing in a corner, watching her.

Ariadne's Labyrinths

In the darkness of Eros' house, we remember our bodies.

There is a song that hails Eros as the Limb Loosner, but he has been much more than that for us. Perverse desires dismembered us long ago; now we're the mere memory of the Cretan women, voices hanging in the air through which Psyche walks.

It's as well she can't see us. Imagine walking down these marble corridors and meeting two hanged women and someone who died in labour bearing a half-bull. The bravest would run away, and sensibly too.

I was twelve when my mother, Pasiphae, fell in love with the bull. Strictly speaking, it was my father who ruined my mother, not Poseidon. Minos, my niggardly and devious father. I have no such excuse. I went wide-eyed and willing into Theseus' arms and when he left me on the beach at Naxos I had only myself to blame.

Minos' mother, my grandmother, was Europa. Carried away by a milk-white bull with dewlaps like sails and horns as pert and delicate as a boy's penis. It was Zeus in disguise. He carried her to Crete – imagine it, a girl who had never been further than the bottom of her father's fields and never, ever alone, suddenly on the trackless ocean with only a bull beneath her and the soaked clothes on her back. She slid off his shoulders on the beach at Karoumes and lay shaking on the sand, where God proceeded to rape her. He was, apparently, so eager that he was still half-bull, half-man, when it was all over and he was gone.

My father got drunk one night and added parts to the story that we had never heard before. Lying on the sand, shaking and in shock (he said), his mother watched her maidenly blood and Zeus' divine sperm trickle out and fill the convolutions left by lugworms. From this site came the idea of the labyrinth – intricate, endless, indivisible from the thing which created it - this sight penetrated Europa as deeply as had Zeus. Minos and the labyrinth, twin castings of a divine lugworm.

Minos grew up mostly alone, except for Europa, who never recovered from her encounter with divine desire. He named himself king of the island and set about building a palace at Knossos. He said he did it for his mother, who felt safe in the maze of corridors, store-rooms, strange sanctuaries which appeared in illogical places, rooms with no purpose, and passages which resisted all attempts to map them. I have a vague memory of my grandmother; white-haired and wild-eyed, suffering night terrors about a thing with horns pursuing her down the tightest of secret passages. It's possible that my father wasn't lying. For once.

If the labyrinth was the outworking of Minos' twisty soul, it didn't stop him attracting my mother, Pasiphaë. Although in many respects a conventional woman, a part of her was attracted to the coils of Minos' devious mind. As I said, Poseidon ruined Pasiphaë, but the seed had been planted by Minos at the beginning of their marriage. Taken to the marital bed when she was practically still a child Minos sowed in her a crop of stories about bulls, gods, and desire. He claimed that his *hamartia* over the bull was due to his mother, Europa. There's no point dissecting it now; Minos' stories were full of dead ends and false trails. Either way, he cheated Poseidon of a milk-white bull and the god retaliated by afflicting my mother with lust for it.

Did her passion for the bull come on fast or slow? How do you woo a bull? How did she even describe the task to Daedalus, the partner of my father's fertile and foxy mind? Although we are all just voices now, my mother still will not talk about it. I burn to know what she thought inside the wooden cow, her legs slotted into its hollow hind ones, her sex thrust up and open to the mighty pizzle. I get no answer, although I have felt a blush in the dark.

I should have asked Minos how he could have been ignorant of what was going on, since he and Daedalus were so thick. How could none of my mother's women have spilled the beans about Pasiphae's obscenity, the dishonor to which she had exposed her children? By the time I realized that Minos had actually wanted to watch a woman mate with bull, to see something like his own awful conception, my mother was dead and I was burning for Theseus.

She died in labour with my brother, whom a vicious posterity has called Minotaur, but whom she named Asterion. He was a beautiful baby – bull-calf, whatever you like. A curling forelock and melting eyes in the massy head which broke my mother's pelvis and killed her before he had been swaddled. He was nursed by a cow from Minos' herd, but he slept in a cradle of olive-wood, carved for a prince. Quite what my father's feelings were for Asterion, I could never determine. The man-bull who was his other self, born from a combination of desire, violence, and stratagem – I couldn't see how Minos could *not* love that.

Not that it mattered, because as Minos aged and Asterion grew, both their tempers worsened. Thus was my brother penned in the maze which replicated the unmappable corridors of Minos' house.

How could we, my sister Phaedra and I, raised in such a house, fail to run a few degrees off true? Desiring a foreigner, desiring your stepson – these are paltry offences compared to our parents' bestial, warped games.

My father made me Asterion's keeper, mistress of the labyrinth. I hated it. It was my job to conduct the Athenian sacrifices to the labyrinth and shut the gate on them. In the beginning most of them died of thirst ten feet from the gate, unwilling to go any further in. My father had Daedalus add a series of traps which forced them towards the centre. We went in to retrieve the remains and to feed Asterion the vegetables which were all he could eat with his bull's teeth. He looked at us from his filth and fury and asked with his great liquid eyes why we did this to him. His man's gut longed for meat, but his bull's head could only eat cabbage and hay, and so he lived in a wretched state of unsated hunger, anger, and darkness.

I wanted out of my father's house, off Crete, and away from my miserable post as gaoler to my mother's abortion. I gave Theseus the ball of twine and dared him to find my centre. I asked him to kill Asterion quickly, and to bring back no trophies. But he did bring back the soft curling forelock which had crowned my brother as a baby. He tied it with the rest of the twine and hung it around my neck. I clutched it in one hand as Theseus towed me along with the other, down to the waiting boat and away from moonlit Knossos.

The rest is predictable: Theseus wanted to return to Athens and reshape the city in his own image. I realized that another encounter between a man and a bull had produced a second Minos. We quarreled; I cried; he left. The last I saw of him was his heroic shoulder, shoving the rowboat off the shallows at Naxos, going back to the ship. Panic flared up for a brief moment before I gave up, realizing that only destiny is stronger than desire. Though it's helpful when they work together.

Between them, desire and destiny have a limited pattern-book. On a beach because of a bull and a boy's desire, I too was raped by a god. Dionysus calls it marriage, but they always do. It's part of Dionysus' gift to make time disappear; being permanently off your face will do that to you. So twelve years later I experienced a brief moment of sobriety – surrounded by strangers whom I was told were my own children – and could no longer bear to be the butt of divine desire.

My brother's forelock hung much heavier around my neck than the noose. It took only seconds to hang myself; I remember thinking that I hung like a bunch of grapes from the vine yet Dionysus was nowhere to be seen.

I didn't choose to spend my afterlife here in the House of Desire; but I would have come anyway and demanded houseroom from the god whose workings so thoroughly ruined us. As it is, I came to find my mother here and my sister Phaedra about to join us.

Poor Phaedra struggled harder than any of us and ended up the same way, her feet describing the cardinal points as she dangled from a beam in her bedroom. Like our mother, she was the victim of another silly man's attempt to cheat the gods. That said, I've never quite found it within me to blame Hippolytus. A prig, a prude, a teenager blinded by anger, but still - he wasn't entirely wrong.

Hippolytus, the son of Theseus (yes, my Theseus, in another of his post-Naxos adventures) and the Amazon Hippolyta. Understandably, the boy burned with anger at his illegitimacy. A bastard can never make headway in the world because an old act of desire between two strangers permanently hobbles him.

Desire terrified Hippolytus. Imagine a child recognizing that there is a force which maddens people and generates new beings, trapping them until they too are impelled to repeat the same mistake. Hippolytus loved the hunt as way out of that consuming desire which makes life. Instead of creating, he released things from the inconvenience of being.

He refused to fulfil his duty to Aphrodite. Enraged, she caused my sister, his stepmother, to lust after him. Phaedra turned into a desperate, sex-obsessed woman, who thirsted for perverse, overheated things.

And here's the thing that Phaedra finds hardest to accept, even now that blame is pointless, and we are only the memories of our most self-abasing acts: Aphrodite used her not because desire was foreign to Phaedra's nature but *because* it was fundamental to it. I hanged myself because I'd had enough, she because she could never have enough.

Why did she marry Theseus, after his dreadful treatment of me? I've asked but get no answer. I wonder if it's *because* of how he treated me. She saw that he was fueled by desire and recognized a natural partner. Thus is the way of siblings – different versions of the same person. Still, Theseus did treat women like a ring dance in a village square: drop hands, one step to the left, begin again. Not that I'm bitter.

In Theseus Phaedra saw the only way out of the maelstrom of her own desire. Marriage is the only path acceptable to a sensual woman who still wants nice clothes, a good table, a soft bed, and the eventual subsuming of desires into the pleasures of old age. When he did his usual disappearing act, she was left as open as a sail to the wind, and Aphrodite drove her mercilessly. A boat built for speed runs before the gale until the sheets snap, the sails rip, and the hull meets the rocks which were always, always waiting for it.

So here we are, Eros' victims in one way or another, drifting about his dark halls remembering desire, which always feels to us like the hot breath of a bull.

Pastos

Psyche has floated into Cupid's world, walked into his house, entered his bed. In the dark she hears his footfall, sees his outline against the open window and the bed's nuptial curtain and hopes that he will not speak.

He parts the curtain, draws back the sheet, and gets into bed beside her. He smells of cinnamon, warmth, and something massy. He turns on his side and rests on one elbow, facing her in the dark, and stretches out a tentative hand. She feels it slide into her hair, around her neck, and draw her towards him.

She fights the urge to giggle. The only time a boy kissed her – Polynices, her father's ward from Boetia – she was nine and he was so nervous he farted. Then she comes within the nimbus of warmth and breath from his lips and the urge to laugh passes. Their lips touch briefly, firmly, then part. Now he is no longer a stranger.

He lets go of her neck and they are separate in the bed. There is silence and she feels a sense of waiting, then realizes that he is inviting her to reciprocate. Even naked and in the strange bed of a strange man, manners prove stronger than any other instinct, and she moves forward again.

Then stops. And for the first time Psyche asks herself calmly whether she wants to kiss him. She decides she doesn't know, and stares off into the darkness of a long moment thinking about it. She feels him smiling in the dark, and this decides her. Psyche slides back towards this strange man, whom an incredible turn of events has made her husband, and returns his kiss like a cormorant diving for a fish.

And in the dark it is Cupid's turn to hold back a laugh. And while he is trying not to laugh at her, Psyche is exploring each crevice of his invisible face. Cupid is kneaded and stroked, poked, licked, and nuzzled by a teenage girl who suddenly has a new toy and no nursemaid to restrain her play. She moves to his neck and chest, finding new heat and textures that lips and fingerpads and teeth and nose-tips have never known.

And eventually she uses her legs for arms, her breasts for fingers, and twines herself around him like Salmacis in the pool, consuming him entirely. She allows him to show her the angle at which things work better, and that he is not a water pump. Eventually, diagonal to where they started, with the pastos hanging crookedly and one pillow left on the bed, she pushes him into the wet patch, steals the pillow, and falls asleep in a lordly sprawl on the bed.

Dawn comes, Cupid staggers away, and in the grove beyond the house there is the sound of a young man giving himself up to laughter. When the light finally wakes Psyche, she finds him gone and the sun high in the sky. She looks at the sheets without emotion and realizes that she must make this her home. There is now no way back over the mountains.

Metamorphosis

A pastos has been hung around the bed. Within it, Cupid can see the outline of the girl, kneeling up in the sheets, not quite ready to spring but not relaxed either. Halfway to the bed, he stops himself, wishing to savour the beauty of the moment.

He has done this thousands of times; it is part of his nature never to lose interest, or to feel that it has grown old or stale. Naiad, dryad, girl, goddess, boy, even birds, beasts, and once, uniquely, a fish. But never in the same shoes as a million nervous, rapacious bridegrooms. He has never parted the wedding curtains before or looked on the face of his bride in the moonlight.

A voice comes from behind the fluttering sarcenet. 'Are you afraid?' she asks.

Although he has gazed long and intimately at Psyche from the heavens, he has not heard her speak. Now he is surprised. Her voice is deep, authoritative; it is the voice of a woman not easily given to fear.

'I was about to ask you the same thing,' he says.

A low laugh. 'Come and find out.'

He parts the pastos and makes his speech. Here, he tells her, she will lack nothing. She will be the mistress of his home and of him, though she must never act upon her curiosity and seek to see his face.

'I see.' She tucks a lock of hair behind his ear and draws him into a kiss. He removes the fibulae which pin her peplos at the shoulders, and reveals breasts more glorious than the moon outside, so generous and unassailable are they.

Awed, he falls back, aware that his instinct to worship this girl is the final insult to his mother. He grasps the fine girdle beneath the peplos and ungirds his young wife. Like an eel she wriggles out of the folds and lies revealed to Cupid.

In the shadows at the apex of her slender legs he sees what even he could not have guessed. Her genitalia resemble the weapons of a soldier: the complexity of a rounded labia is her hoplon, and in it is couched a rearing doru, a long-handled and recurved penis. Again he falls back, awed that this girl, whom he has desired for her beauty, should possess completeness as well. Now he understands her name, which alludes to the part beyond, or before, gender.

She wraps her legs around his waist and draws him to the hot centre which precedes everything. He recalls Salmacis encircling unwilling Hermaphroditus in the pool, dragging him to a fatal synthesis, fusing him to herself forever. Just such absorption is in Psyche's nature: male and female, now human and divine.

Reflexion

Lying in the dark with Psyche in his arms, the god feels her thinking. So far she has abided by his only rule, not to seek a glimpse of his face.

But her thinking puzzles him, this silent process he has seen in humans and some animals. Human thought is to the gods like those fish which change sex, or eels which generate from mud – an oddity of no real consequence. Gods do not think. They act and they desire. They definitely do not think about themselves. If they were to do this, it would emanate another universe, with other gods.

But Psyche is thinking about herself, and feeling certain things about these thoughts. He asks nonetheless, because he sees – a bit sadly – that this is at the heart of being human, which is what the gods would like to understand most of all.

'What is it like to think about yourself?'

She pauses, and he feels her trying to explain something he will never know.

'You are alone in a clearing at night with a forest on all sides. Wishing to escape the brightness of the night, in which you feel a huge and terrifying clarity peering at you, you move into the trees. At first the forest seems fragrant, soft with moss and sleep. The deep blues and thick blackness soothe your star-jangled nerves. You walk deeper and deeper among the trunks. At your back you hear a noise more deliberate than the woods' gentle respiration.

'You stop to focus on the sound. What is its nature – a footfall? A man carrying weapons? A woman or child lost in the woods? Or worse, not lost in the woods?

'You begin to move faster and faster, but this only makes your pursuer move faster too. Your heart is racing; flight is all your fear-narrowed mind can think; the terrible connection your pursuer has with you is unbreakable.

'To catch your breath you stop, sobbing, pressing your face into the wet moss of a tree, and you understand that it is your pursuer's awful potential in all this directionless darkness that terrifies you. You do not know what he wants, or how you can give it to him even if you have it, or what the meaning of this trial might be.

'Overhead the moon passes. You catch a glimpse of your own hand, shaking and bleeding, on a branch. You realize that your pursuer is yourself, and the forest a darkness into which you have willingly walked. You cannot return to the clearing, and the fear will not abate.'

Limits

Every morning the world is made anew. Asleep, entwined in the arms of her god, the girl does not see it happen. As far as she is concerned the world now consists of a few places, joined up by her own experience.

There is Bed, which is part of Night and Him. In Bed, Sleep happens, or no Sleep, depending on His mood. During Day she knows House and Grove. At the far end of Grove, there is Cliff on one side, Forest on two others, and River on the last. These are the limits of her world.

Once she tried to imagine what might happen if these things were paired differently: Bed and Him in Day, the Grove at Night, or River and Darkness. She began to feel sleepy. She tried to push through this torpor and found questions: where is He in the Day? Home, Memories – do they exist somewhere else? If He is not here, is there no Night? She slept for a long time after that, and that Night He was insistent that she relinquish thoughts of who she once was and what was possible.

She waits until He is asleep and leaves the bed.

She closes the bedroom door behind her and finds the house dark but still present, the corridor and front door where they always are. She goes outside and sees the river and the moon, and realizes the pairings are not quite immutable, just that her experience has been very circumscribed.

She walks on and reaches the grove, where she turns a full circle under the moon, looking up at the silvery cliff, the dense shadows of the forest. Up against this border of what she knows, she discovers that she can now think clearly. What does he do when he is not with her? Where does he come to her from? Who is he, that he can so completely engineer her world and what she knows?

She reaches the river, hikes up her skirt and plunges in tentatively. Cold river water swallows her feet, her ankles, and eventually her thighs. She pushes on, the water lapping breast high, but the silvery expanse seems to widen indefinitely before her. She retreats and stands knee-high in water looking over to the other bank. The moonlight is bright, but the far bank remains an indistinct black bar and it suddenly occurs to her that she cannot remember what it looks like in daylight – if she has ever known.

She turns back, wades ashore, and sits for a while. Still wet, she walks to the first rows of trees on the other side of the grove, her feet sinking into a deep moss that muffles all sound. The moon still sails overhead, but it shows only a forest of the most generic kind, black bars of trees, a half-thought-out canopy, and neither animal nor bird to break the unnatural silence. After some hours of walking straight ahead, she sees a clearing, and emerges in the grove where she started. The night has not advanced by even a moment.

He stands in the shadow of the columns, waiting for her to finish exploring the limits of her world, and leads her back to Bed.

Mirror

After months without the sight of another face, Psyche is desperate to see her own. She rises from bed and goes to find a mirror. She rouses the servants and demands a light. Her husband pads up, barefoot, behind her and dismisses the servants.

'Why do you need to see yourself?'

'I can't love you if I'm no longer sure I even exist.'

'Isn't being loved proof enough?'

'Then why have eyes?'

'This will end everything.'

Angered, she says, 'Then it is slavery, not love. Only slaves are not permitted to know themselves.'

There is a moment of silence, and Psyche feels the reality of her position. She has known that this body who enfolds her every night is Cupid. If you can accept that the gods speak through an oracle, demand your death, catch you as you fall from a mountain, and lead you to a place peopled by invisible servants, it's hardly a stretch to accept that one of these forces shares your bed and your body.

She wants to see herself. She wants to see how he has changed her. She can no longer remember what she looked like, and this frightens her. Thoughts and memories once securely bundled in a notion of herself are leaching out like bread soaked in milk. There is no clear start to her and end to the clothes she wears, the wind which touches her, the food she eats or the couches she lies on. All the otherness of the world is held back by the little dam-wall of her reflection.

She suspects that her invisible husband wants to immerse her in the endless synthesis of everything, to show that the world is a fluid unity and boundaries are a trick of the mind reinforced by names. She wants the illusion of a firm and certain self back, and for this she needs a mirror and a light.

'I'm begging you. I haven't begged for anything before,' he says. 'Do not do this.'

'Give me a light.'

At first she sees only her eyes, then she gauges how much she has been consumed. The light he radiates shows embers in the shape of a girl, still glowing. A black drift of cinders has begun. She stares at the crumbling ash of herself. She lifts a hand to wipe away tears and scatters parts of her face, her head. She turns to strike him, and collapses in a powdery heap at his feet.

Loneliness

You only have a brief window of time in which to cure loneliness, like handling a coal without getting burned. It is a kind of falling through space; you cannot stop yourself. Some other force must supervene, but it is precisely that force which has put you here.

Psyche is a specimen in a bell jar of divine love, forbidden to look at the face beyond the glass.

They live like this for some months: two shapes in the dark exchanging heat, knowing everything and nothing about each other. It is evident that one of them is divine, but quite which one is uncertain from moment to moment. Until one night Cupid comes to bed and warns her not to listen to the crying which drifts over the mountains.

'Why would I?'

There is a pause. 'I don't know. Just don't.'

'What is it?'

A longer pause. She realizes he is kicking himself for bringing this up.

'Your sisters. They mourn you.'

She closes her mouth tightly. 'What would they do here anyway?'

'It doesn't matter. If they come, it'll be the end of things.' He draws her down to the pillow.

It is a splinter in their strange life.

Cupid is incensed by her loneliness. When she cries he sees the world as it appears to the human beings with whom he plays as he whiles away eternity.

Predictably, the argument begins in the bedroom. The body he adores has congealed around a handkerchief and no arms reach out to him in the darkness. Her sniffles infuriate him. Acidly, he says, 'Is this what I can expect from my wife?'

'I'm not your wife. Wives have sisters to visit. Wives see their husbands. I don't know who you are. I don't even know that you're the same person from night to night.'

He ignores the idea that marriage requires a degree of visibility. 'You'll regret this.'

Snuffles. 'What.'

'Having your sisters here.'

There is a pause. 'Really?' She doesn't mean really-I'll-regret-this? but really-I-can-have-my-sisters?

'It'll destroy everything. They will make you look at my face.' He realizes that to Psyche nothing is worth having if she can't show it to someone. Some remote part of him finds it amusing. She has true communion with the divine, wealth, a beauty untainted by age, the very forces of earth and air at her command, and she will endanger it all to see sisters whom he knows hate her.

'Really?' She swears vows he has never asked of her; things she has never needed to say. She swears she would rather face a hundred deaths than endanger this strange half-union she has only just described as a farce.

'I love you, desperately,' she says into his neck. Her voice cracks with happiness at the thought of her sisters and his heart breaks a little. She breathes in. 'I love you, whoever you are. I love you as my own life. I hold you higher than Desire itself.' He hears this, most self-abasing declaration from the girl he has put through death and fear and loneliness, and even he, the god, feels ashamed.

'Just...'

'Just what.'

'Just let me command the Zephyr. Bring them here as you brought me.'

But he is no longer interested. The future has just clarified itself and gained a new weight. It feels like a ring on his finger, close-fitting, inevitable. 'Of course.'

'Really?' And she is upon him, legs everywhere like a spaniel, and he catches her heat and wetness, like the scent of a new apple, and he is lost.

Prophecies

Somewhere, a nightingale is singing.

In a Trojan temple a brown-haired girl bares herself to Apollo and invites a trade: her body for the gift of prophecy.

From the shadows he appears. Loitering behind a potted laurel-tree. He comes forward, and she sees the god whose eyes are the colour of the future. She does not yet know that lies are a device to separate us from others.

Stepping up to him she offers her lips as his mouthpiece. She takes one long-fingered, lyre-player's hand and places it on her breast. He casts a speculative look at her in the long shards of moonlight, and the transaction is made. Like gossamer, the future is now imprinted on her eyes; wherever she looks she will see things yet to be and forestall or hasten them with a word. She will have the power to set gods and men against each other and to frustrate the designs of both.

Apollo has given her prophetic powers, but not a mirror. She will see the future of everyone but herself. And this is why, as he closes the space between them to claim her, she puts a cool hand on his chest and stops him.

In the years of agony which will follow, years as a prisoner and a concubine until the knife of her captor's treacherous wife slides between her ribs, Cassandra will wonder what possessed her to refuse him. It is, of course, a trick of Apollo's. Much less motivated by sex than sheer stratagem, he could not allow the design in the weave to be given away. The future, with all its sea-battles and topless towers, must remain unknown because in that ignorance lies the gods' power.

She explains, smugly, that she has sworn a vow of virginity. He acquiesces, which should have warned her, and asks for a single kiss.

Uptilted, her lips meet his, cool and divine. They part briefly and she feels the flicker of his tongue, like a serpent's whisper. He grasps her chin and her mouth falls open to his, greedy for more than prophetic words.

In the quiet temple, Apollo spits in the mouth of the girl he is kissing.

The future rolls on, Cassandra reels back, and the gift is tainted.

Cassandra will recognize Helen as a disaster the moment she sees her. She will foretell the fall of Troy. And no one will believe her.

Apollo steps back into the shadows and is gone, leaving Cassandra to rape and rejection, captivity and murder. The spit sits on her tongue until she swallows.

Cassandra, made mad because she cannot tell a lie. Psyche, sorrowful in her golden house with her archer-armed husband, appalled that soon she will have to lie.

Summons

In the same week both of Psyche's sisters, separated by marriage and mountains, have similar dreams. They write letters to each other – they work out later that the runners probably passed through the same narrow defile within half a day of each other.

Although it is always summer in the House of Desire, in the kingdoms of men the harvest is in and stubble fires smoke in the fields. Perhaps the cindery smell has entered their dreams as they sleep beside their old and infirm husbands. Either way, the sisters dream of harvest nights when they were girls and Psyche was tiny.

One writes:

I have dreamt of the polecat we kept years ago. In the dream we are again garlanded and dancing around the harvest fires, summoning the dark lady. Through her eyes we see the Maiden taken. When we were young the Maiden was faceless, just screams becoming fainter as the All-Embracer took her away.

I have seen her face.

The other writes:

I dreamed that we rode father's black horses around the bounds of his kingdom, and Hekabe ran, barking, at our heels. We reached the edge of the forest and a stag bounded out; the horses reared and Hekabe sprang forward. Among the shadows of the trees I saw white-armed Iphigenia step back, replaced beneath the knife by a deer.

The sisters meet, alone and with garlands in hand, at the rock where Psyche was left. The two queens sit with their skirts hiked up and dangle their feet into space. Over a golden horizon white clouds blow like a child blowing sycamore seeds down a stream. They hold hands and cry for all the things that sisters cry about: past time, the unfairness of things, the gap between what they hoped for and how things turned out, and how pudgy little Psyche, whom they took to the rites of Hecate, grew into a woman and was assailed by life.

They are crying companionably when the breeze in the canyon carries the sound of a girl's voice. It is more than Psyche calling; it is years wasted in dutiful marriages, and the lure of things now soured made right again. 'Let the wind take you!'

They look at each other, afraid that the voice is a shared delusion calling them to death.

'Trust me!' It is undeniably Psyche.

Without waiting for them to screw up their courage, the Zephyr seizes them in a screaming tangle of tunics and veils and paddling feet. Psyche's sisters fly to her in Cupid's summery bell-jar. They fall on each other, crying and laughing all at once, smelling familiar skin, feeling the arms of childhood. Psyche feels time regain its elastic character now that her sisters are here. Time, the force to which her husband will never succumb.

Yet from the second they break away from Psyche's embrace, they are all pretending. Her sisters do not ask how she comes to be commanding winds, or what this place is, so close to their home and yet as different as an underwater world. And true to her contract with Cupid, Psyche offers no explanation of how she was drawn from a cliff's edge into marriage with the owner of the golden house.

She leads her sisters through the gardens to the glittering stoa. Its crassness makes her blush – though her sisters just finger the fluted columns thoughtfully and look at their little sister as if she was holding out on them. She tugs them towards the bath, where they are attended by the same disembodied servants. She laughs as they start at the pitchers and towels floating through the air – and blushes when her sisters ask immediately what took her days to think of: what are these invisible servants concealing?

The day passes and Psyche discovers how good it is for human eyes to rest on other human figures, and how much passes wordlessly between family. She realizes that once they are safe, humans turn their attention to gain, and almost dies of shame at her avaricious sisters' thirst for the treasure rooms.

Her sisters, their hands dripping gold as if they had disemboweled Midas, demand who he is, this husband who has so little respect for wealth. Psyche realizes that she must do an entirely new thing: she must lie.

He's a hunter, she says. *He hunts. Animals. Hunting. He's young, only my age, barely bearded. But handsome. And the wealth's inherited.*

Standing in pools of treasure with their hard eyes on her, Psyche suddenly wants her sisters gone. She puts a golden breastplate in her eldest sister's hand and turns away.

You should go, she says. She can feel him in the shadows, watching them.

They ask, *Can we come back?*

They are already speaking through the filmy veil of different desires and private thoughts. She is walking them to the door, clinking as they scoop up golden beads and baubles which strain their skirts.

Yes, yes. The zephyr will bring you. You can trust it; you won't fall.

And indeed the zephyr is waiting, a polite funnel of moving air. It expands around them like a chariot wall of wind, and after the first breathless shrieks her sisters fall silent and look back at Psyche, growing smaller below them. She watches them go and turns away, unhappy that the world and wealth have cut adrift what remained of her childhood.

None of them have used the word *god.*

Comparisons

For a long time the eldest sister says nothing. She walks away from the cliff edge with one tremendous wish: that she had not seen any of it. Not Psyche, not the golden house, nor the treasure, nor the traces of the god to whom her youngest sister is clearly married.

This is how it begins, the souring of the sisterhood: something about a woman offends them *as* women. A shared nature isn't the basis for a society, but rather shared desires. Not competing ones. Women may have a separate part of the house – it doesn't mean that they're a separate household. Like men, whose brotherhood lasts until the first pretty woman walks past, the idea of a sisterhood is a patina covering up the cracks in a loose confederation of warring states.

The triadic event of seeing, ruining, regretting, which Psyche will soon bring upon herself is pre-empted by her eldest sister. She will turn to the dark-faced holder of the tally stick: Rhamnousia, who lives in the forests of northern Attica and is known elsewhere as Nemesis.

The insult of Psyche's good fortune stings her sister like an insect bite. She looks down at her hands, wrinkled and spotted with chemical burns from poultices and liniments. Her husband is old, arthritic, and uses her as his nurse. She has known a marital embrace precisely four times, and still shudders with the embarrassment of it.

Her eyes fill with tears. She is tired, invisible, and bitterly disappointed in her lot. Why was she born?

Beside her, her middle sister is still churning the tub of her own grumbles. She too is disappointed in marriage; she too is outraged by Psyche's fortune, but it is Psyche's youth that gets her goat.

Something is curdling in the sisters' hearts. They feel themselves blackening inside and it is unstoppable, the way you know you are going to vomit and begin grinding your teeth. They try to feel compassion: *Psyche is our sister and she loves us; would we want this done to us, if the places were reversed? This anger is a bad and wicked thing and no good will come of it; besides, she's not even happy – she lied about her husband and her house is unnatural, for all her wealth.* The objections mass, but both sisters know they are proleptic.

Her elder sister can bear it no longer. 'You can do what you like, but I will not take this lying down. I am sick to death of being the billboard that advertises her. No one will hear about her house, or her husband, or even that she's alive, from me.'

Numb, the other nods. She knows what is coming. When you're about to do something terrible, you first tell the story which justifies it. 'So what will we do?'

'We'll go home. We'll tell no one. We'll grieve for Psyche. And when I've thought of a plan, we will end her.'

Atavism

We had a dog called Ajax when my sisters and I were children. He was a patient, curly-haired lap-dog whom we swaddled and loved until even my mother treated him like a baby. He escaped one summer and ran into the forest. We were astonished. It hadn't occurred to us that our love actually suffocated him. I only saw him once more, just after the first snow separated the house from the forest beyond. Among the trees I caught sight of something big, rough-coated, keen-eyed and wary, and recognized a dog that had once been Ajax.

My father explained that Ajax had returned to the thing he had always been, just as we would if we left settled life and took to the forests again. My younger sisters cried at the thought of his cold, hungry, and likely short life. But I saw that it could be a great relief to return to behaviours that could no longer be swaddled out of you.

When Ajax returned to the forests I asked my mother about the first women: what would we return to if we left the hearth and loom, and the dismal business of babies? She had no answer. Overhearing us, my father said, 'What makes you think women have grown away from their natural state?' He kissed the top of my mother's head, but I saw her flush with anger.

After the war in heaven, the first war on earth was between the stories of men and those of women. In men's stories we're given neither the time nor talent for friendship. Our stories, like captives, have been bred with theirs and are slowly betraying us.

Here is a man's story about women.

The gods gave Prometheus and his brothers an earth teaming with game, but no means to smelt iron for weapons to kill it or ways to cook it. Men looked at each other and saw exhaustion from running down the quarry, madness from beating it to death with a wooden club, and the revulsion of tearing it raw and dripping.

Prometheus decided to steal fire.

It is pointless to ask how he knew such a thing existed. He did, that's all – and in that sentence is most of life. I am inclined to think well of Prometheus despite all that followed, because he was simply solving an unbearable situation. Asking someone to accept less than what's possible – this is what gods do to us, and then watch us spiral into madness and death.

Through fire men came together around a hearth, and that meant competition. In their version of the story, men say they were lonely because fire demands to be shared. Embraces between men might comfort, but they yield no new life. They became aware that they lacked something which could not be stolen.

They asked the gods for something to cure the loneliness. To requite Prometheus' theft, the gods gave them a left-handed gift. A woman.

Down she came from heaven, with the hornet's nest between her legs and the jar of evils in her hands. A profound and complete trap, Pandora redressed the balance which Prometheus' theft had knocked askew.

Looked at one way, a woman is on a par with fire as a force to change things. Looked at another, it took fire to make men godlike, and woman to reduce them to beasts.

What goes on four legs at dawn, two at noon, and three at dusk? A woman's idea of herself, given by men.

Picture it: the jar she's been told not to open. The curiosity which burns her as badly as Prometheus' sense of what men could achieve. A crowd of horrified hypocrites shouting at her that it has been forbidden. And after the evils have flown out, hope.

Here is a woman's version of the story.

Pandora opened her eyes for the first time and saw a crowd of expectant men. She felt the jar she had been given to carry. Heard her first word: *Don't.* The men, who made clear to her that she was not like them and was entirely alone on this new earth of cooking smells and clanging weapons, fought over her. She learned about injuries and competition.

The jar intrigued her and worried her. Either it contained something worse than the large, violent, demanding creatures around her, or something better. It might contain something what made her feel less alone. She began to despair and opened the jar. At the bottom was hope.

She learned that hope follows action and that sooner or later you must look at what's been hidden from you.

With the arrival of more women, Pandora realized that they were all captives whose suffering separated them from each other. Hamstrung by bodies which betrayed them on a dismal, cyclical basis, and imprisoned by terrifying, uncontrolled replication, a woman's function was to multiply and her character shaped by curiosity and treachery equally. This is the type we return to, like a dog turning his back on the hearth and the caresses of children.

You may say, embrace your sister and so halve your resentment at Psyche's good fortune. Co-operate and prosper. Do not let the stories of men tell you what you are.

But I have no talent for friendship. I cannot pity Psyche as a woman because she offends me as a woman. I cannot love her as a sister because sisters are doubles, and stories cannot cope with doubles. Like Ajax rejecting our caresses, I cannot bring myself to overcome my anger at my sister's fortune. So I return to type, the deep and total trap which stories have told me I always was.

Periphery

My wife was the eldest of three sisters. Twenty years younger than me. Radiant. Demanding. Jealous.

A singer came to the house in the depths of winter. Over ten nights he sang the travels of Odysseus returning from Troy. I lay in bed with my wife and she asked me in which character I most saw myself.

I considered carefully; I knew the answer would confuse her. When was confused she became spiteful. Still, I said, 'Dolius, the gardener.'

She raised herself on one elbow to look at me. Her hair fell in a shining curtain over her silken shoulders. 'The slave?'

I laughed. Despite her disgust she was so beautiful that I moved closer to kiss the hollow of her shoulder. She stiffened and I saw her skin rise and gooseflesh with revulsion. I drew back to my own side. 'Is it so surprising? He survives. He is the father of six fine boys and a daughter. He recognizes Odysseus when he returns and fights on his side against the suitors.'

'But he's a slave! He's a nobody in the story. How can you see yourself as someone so…peripheral?' She tasted the word as if it were a bad piece of fruit.

I felt the difference in our ages. 'Being peripheral usually means surviving to tell about all the glory-seekers who died.' I saw that this meant nothing to her. At twenty, how can you understand dying?

She fell back on the pillow and was asleep in moments. I watched her, sleeping the easy, total sleep of the young. My beautiful wife, eldest of three beautiful girls. Sister of a girl so ridiculously beautiful that her parents had to atone for it. I thought about my in-laws. Not one of that entire drama-prone family could understand the deep and abiding happiness that comes from drawing absolutely no attention.

The longer you live the more it seems a gift, this being peripheral. It has the benefits of prophecy without the madness, and invisibility without the inconvenience. You can see a great action from a sidelong position, and nobody cares whether you live or die. Every story is an epitaph to its main characters, but the minor figures establish the limits of the heroes' world. The future belongs to you.

Certainly, nobody chooses to be peripheral. It's not even thrust upon you. You just realize (and this is the definition of middle age) that this is how you are: marginal, unimportant, minor in every way. Nobody can remember whether you attended their wedding or not, and when some singer names the war-dead of your generation it occurs to you that you're still alive. Some people would be peripheral even in their own story. In a Doliad, a (short, quiet) epic entirely focused on the deeds of Dolius, Odysseus' gardener, he would still end up on the edge of the action.

So my wife had another reason to curl her lip at me, as if my age, my baldness, my prudence, our quiet court, weren't enough. She took to calling me Dolius, until I warned her that mocking me was likely to end badly for her. She chafes for some great, bright light, despite the example of her younger sister. Trapped in a penumbral marriage, she envies even the memory of Psyche. I foresee that her unhappiness will result in rash things, spiteful things, and not even those will catapult her to the centre.

Obviously, there are disadvantages to being peripheral: your feelings are either forgotten or ignored, and the idea of your name surviving eternity is ridiculous. But at some point the heroes beg for it. When you can no longer bear yourself but lack the energy to end it, you long for the slow orbit of the periphery, quietly bringing you to your centre, not your edge.

Historia

Your Majesties,

Having sent me to discover what became of your wives, their majesties the queens of your lands, I send you the account of my findings.

Although you believed that your wives had gone on a pilgrimage of mourning for a younger sister, this turned out to be untrue. Or at least, not true in the way that men mean it, but women, as your majesties doubtless know, twist the relation of word to thing until it is chimerical. When we say, 'I am going on a pilgrimage to mourn my younger sister,' built into that claim, as a sword to its scabbard, is the assurance that there was a younger sister, existing in the same way as the speaking *I*, and that this younger sister has now died.

Alas, such simplicity is not the way of women. Several weeks of enquiry established that your wives never had a sister, younger or otherwise. When they left your respective borders with only a brawny maidservant each for protection, they went directly to the mountainous region of their parents' kingdom, and met in a well-known pass which opens onto a rocky theatre with a sheer drop to the valley below.

I hid in a cave higher up and looked down as they clasped each other, weeping and loosing their hair in what seemed genuine grief. Together they went to the edge of the cliff and it was only the two maidservants' lack of alarm that prevented me from rushing down to stop them from throwing themselves off.

Their actions had the curious, smooth quality of ritual. They bared their breasts to the gusts which race up and down the valley. It seemed that they were inviting the wind, or something on the wind, to take them away. At times I heard the word *psyche* shouted, in tones of grief, and invitations to eros to come on the wind and take this psyche away.

At nightfall they retired to camp in a narrow defile. I spent a cold night listening to the talk of foolish women, who complained about each of your majesties and the loveless toil that took up their days. It became clear that *psyche* referred not to a younger sibling, but to a kind of women's *daimon*, like the soul which men have. From their conversation, I gathered that they regarded their marriages as having sacrificed this psyche, which they now sought to revive by a union with eros. At this point I almost withdrew and wrote to assure you that nothing more than a woman's ritual lay behind the ladies' absence. The maidservants' reference to Corinth gave me pause, however.

At dawn they turned south and I followed them at a half-day's distance until they fell in with other women making for the temple at Corinth. Inquires revealed that these women all believed themselves to be suffering from a sacrificed psyche, and sought to reunite this aspect (I only use their words, my lords, and you should not believe that I subscribe to the notion of women being made in the same manner as a man) with eros through rites at the Corinthian temple of Aphrodite Pandemos.

I will spare your majesties the details of the ladies' deeds at Corinth. Suffice to say that you are not alone in being cuckolded (many times) in the name of religion, and that many other prominent men will welcome sons not their own into their homes, because their wife mourned the death of a fictional younger sister. It was in this manner, I believe, that the ladies accumulated the golden jewellery with which they returned.

I might also add here that my own participation in these rites was entirely for investigative purposes, and it is in that spirit that I send my complements to both ladies, and to your majesties.

Sisyphus

He's like Sisyphus, Psyche thinks. His rock is his thing. Or in Cupid's case, it's railing about her sisters. She notices that his divinity is now accepted between them. How did something like godhead end up like crockery on a dresser – mute, background, but still smashable?

He's telling her that even now her sisters are lying to their mother. His mouth shapes the same lies they tell, as they tell them in the world beyond the valley. If he wasn't so repetitive, this simultaneity would be fascinating. But Cupid hectors and Psyche promises, and both dig themselves deeper into the positions that marriage and habit have made for them.

He rolls the boulder up: *your sisters are she-wolves, faithless, duplicitous, driven by their need to bring you down.* He rolls the boulder down: *they'll tempt your curiosity, the one thing I know you can't control. They'll make you look upon my face.*

Listening idly, Psyche recalls that Sisyphus also tested his wife's love. On the brink of death he decided that it was the ideal time to see how obedient she was. Could she overcome her reverence for convention and leave his body unburied in the marketplace, if he ordered her? It seemed not. She had his nagging, demanding, and finally silent body washed and properly buried, and he woke up in the queue for the Styx ferry. Fuming at her disobedience, he made his case to Dis and asked for a brief reprieve to return and chastise her. He enjoyed his stolen time in the upper world so much that he forgot to return. After a lifetime of saying 'Let it be so' to his wife, he ignored Hades' command to return. He was frogmarched to his boulder, and shown the hill up which he would roll it eternally.

Cupid has finished decrying her sisters. He sits on their bed, waiting in the dark. She gives him a willing smile, which hits the wall of his anger and slides down it like an egg.

Later she will see that his stern injunction not to seek a glimpse of his face were more than marital boulder-rolling. Psyche's unhappiness lies in trying to obey the warnings, and her simultaneous knowledge that she will ignore them.

Why does Cupid put her through this? Why make her suffer the contradictions of her own make-up? To force her to resolve them. As a philosopher will later point out, Sisyphus rolls his boulder up and down the hill, entirely content. It's no punishment to him because he's defined by his task, and because his total immersion in boulder-rolling is the measure of his immersion in life. Sisyphus largely missed out on life while he was alive because he refused to commit himself. Always doubting, always outside of himself at an agonizing, critical distance. Finally, he sees life's attractions too late. This is why he can happily roll his boulder: he has made a choice.

Psyche, on the other hand, has not. Brought to love without effort, all she has wanted is her sisters. She's applying a dock leaf to a great gaping wound. Cupid wants to be known. He *wants* Psyche to see that their situation is untenable, ludicrous. A marriage between a kidnapped girl and a faceless man? It is the definition of absurdity. This is the point of all his nagging: to make Psyche conscious of her absurd position.

Frustrated, Cupid ups the ante. He tells her something so obscene, so outrageous, that she should grab him by the curls, haul him into the light, and tell him to be off.

He tells her that she's pregnant. He enfolds this news in a warning and a dilemma. Your sisters will provoke you to look upon my face, he says. Do that and the child will be mortal. Restrain yourself and the child will be divine.

Glossing over for a moment his toe-curling way of putting it: *your childlike womb carries another child like yourself*, how can Psyche ignore this astonishing challenge? How can she fail to miss Cupid's underlying plea? *Divinity is not a state to be sought; that way lies the isolation of limitlessness.*

But Psyche, like the donkey making straight for the roses of illusion, smiles on into the darkness.

Ganymede

Squatting in the dust, two boys play knucklebones. One is losing and resents it. The other does not know how to address his friend's resentment without making it worse. The losing boy is handsome in the keen, restless way of sighthounds and foxes. He tosses the pebbles up, catches most in the hollows of his fist, and watches one, indecisive pebble wobbling on his knuckle. There is a second of strange calm as he gazes at the small stone on his hand, willing it to fall into place. As if moved by an invisible force, the pebble obediently drops into the fleshy hollow.

The boy is a god.

The pebble is just a pebble.

Seeing the blatant use of this unfair power, Ganymede drops his own handful of stones in dismay and stalks off. He is not a god, although he is so beautiful that several deities have offered him divinity if he will only share his perfect lines, his high gold-and-rose colouring, the eyes of Aegean blue, his muscles full from throwing the discus under the sun. Ganymede's beauty is a source of irritation to Cupid.

Seeing Ganymede robbed of victory, a beautiful woman comes over and reprimands Cupid, but lightly – he is, after all, older than she –because she herself has cheated, often and as blatantly as this.

But Ganymede is horrified by the ease with which gods cheat. He sees that they cheat because they belong to a different order of action. His beauty is tainted by anger, the majesty of his stature spoiled by a fear of what heaven allows to happen. In a single moment he has seen the order of things with a merciless clarity.

He hangs himself, the knucklebones scattered beneath his feet.

Cupid cheats Psyche too. Instead of the child he has claimed, she carries an almond kernel in her. If he could have given her a child, he would have, but desire is barren. Its nature is to burn, but not to breed. This explains the confusion over who came first, Eros or Aphrodite, and why Eros always looks like a child.

Day by day Psyche flourishes and it is not until her veins, her throat, her mouth, are filled with the lovely white flowers of the almond blossom, and she has sworn on the Styx never to ask for her sisters again, or to seek the sight of her lover's face, that she realizes that Eros has again cheated his way to victory.

What does she do when she sees this? What can any of us do about that definitively human situation of being beaten by a force which has ignored our rules? Cuddling the belly which is not quite barren but certainly does not carry what she expected, Psyche is gradually brought to ground. Without the panic or the relief of Daphne's metamorphosis into a laurel, Psyche accepts that she would never have won the game. The gods behave according to a different set of laws. You suffer because of a human mania for rules: we want something, and we want it in a particular way. Sometimes we set the way of getting it over the thing itself.

The gods go straight for the thing itself and their disregard for the way they get it is what we experience as life. The indignation and confusion that Psyche feels when her labour pains turn out to be the roots of an almond tree extruding from her, dragging her down to the plot of soil which she will never leave – this awful pain is our desires colliding with the gods'. And our bitterness, even when we are flowering, even when we are a rain of blossoms, comes from the knowledge that the gods will always win.

This is the definition of a god: that possibility which ends up being the case.

Patterns

Foresight lies in recognizing that a story is being told again. Patterns of events are like yeast; once they've set in you can't get rid of them.

Cupid recognizes a familiar pattern of events: a pregnant woman. A god hiding his appearance from her. A rash promise which will threaten her baby.

Semele smiles expectantly. Zeus frowns in an agony of indecision. There is a vivid blue flash, almost too momentary for her human eye to catch. It is a theophany, the god's revelation of his true form, which she has demanded although Zeus has begged her to reconsider.

Facing each other, Semele is still smiling as she crumbles to dust.

The child falls from her womb and is caught by his father, who peels open his thigh and seals the baby into it, where it will gestate until it is born again.

Why do you even want to see God? Seeing will bring you no closer. The divine sits in the centre of a circle – it's the same distance from God to any point in time. Life as you know it is lived on one spoke of the wheel, revolving through what you experience as time.

Like Psyche, Semele wouldn't be told. Lying on a bed overlooking the bay where she had washed off the bull's blood, Zeus had tried again and again to explain the consequences of letting her see him in his true form.

Gods are made to pronounce, not describe. Imagine we agreed to make a suit of clothes – we'd make the jacket four miles across the shoulders and the pants six miles in the leg. We don't think on your scale.

When Cupid watches Psyche cry in unhappy dreams he thinks of the similarity between his warning and Zeus'– *seeing me will bring on disaster. You won't be able to stand it, do you hear? It will destroy you.* He has cursed every one of those unsatisfactory words. For all his godhead, he cannot get down into that tiny space where some magnetic force repels word from thing and close the gap.

Nothing in the living universe is well made; the edges of words aren't flush with each other, there's a barely perceptible unevenness in the foundations, the people are unruly and sometimes unpredictable, even though the gods have cut them in half.

This is the anguish of godhead: to love, to know, and still to hurt from the pain you saw coming.

Lamia

I could smell the child on my sister Psyche before even she knew she was pregnant. This is how it is to be hungry.

The women of my husband's kingdom are superstitious. They will have no sudden visits to their childbed, even from a queen. I do not feed in my own territory, and besides, there is something about the hot, sweet smell of labour blood that sickens me, and the first cries, which fall silent but never really stop.

My husband turned me.

I still sucked my thumb when I married him. He was already old and bitterly arthritic. His sister treated his pains and the two of them were sequestered in his sickroom, mumbling over poultices and unguents. I thought he had forgotten me, but one day my sister-in-law fell, breaking a hip. She died in agony that night, and he sent for me.

I learned how to make the poultices that soothed his joints, which were knotty as burls on a tree. I would take his hand and think that this was what flesh and bone could deform to. His hands and knees were particularly bad; he could only get relief from heat and almost constant massage. With his sister dead I had to supervise the household and make him comfortable enough to deal with greater affairs.

The first winter locked him up entirely. He was a prisoner in his own body and pain made him unbearable. We were snowbound in the great house. After kicking around for the first month his bodyguard was restless and bad-tempered. They took it out first on the women, then on each other, until I took a late-born lamb and slaughtered it in the forest, tearing out its throat and messing the entrails into a bloody circle. Shivering, I painted signs on the snow with the blood. I came back to the house and told the six brawny thugs who couldn't protect my husband from himself that something was in the forest killing the beasts. I suggested that it was worse than wolf or bear, and might move towards the village with evil intent. They made a great fuss of arming themselves and set off happily to gild their own legends.

In peace, I organized the girls into a relay of nurses for my husband, massaging oregano oil into his hands and keeping him in a haze. I expect it did nothing to dull the pain, but it let the house sleep. I moved my bed out of his room and slept among the girls, in whose warmth I tried to find my sisters. It was too late, though. I have never recovered the feeling of my sisters' beds, that snugness of family when time and fate still lay behind a strong curtain wall.

The guard had been gone for ten days when one of the girls died in her sleep. She had been in his sickroom for half the night and went to bed when one of the others relieved her. She was a hale girl of fourteen, with fat honey-coloured braids and a high complexion. When her bed mate went to rouse her in the mid-morning she found a shriveled husk like a dried fig, and the braids fallen out at the roots like an old woman's.

They called me and I went, wondering if she had poisoned herself through the skin with the poultices, or her heart had given way after a night's nursing, but the state of her – ash grey and withered as a sapless branch – suggested something else. It crossed my mind that my fiction about a monster in the forest had invited some lurking winter thing over the threshold, and that the guard was chasing in the snow what I had conjured up among our beds.

There was nothing to do but bury her, forbid the girls from talking about it, and take back the task of nursing the old man myself. In the event, he rallied overnight and was out of bed and actually laughing by dawn. He comforted the girls and told them that a weak heart ran in the dead girl's family. He would never forgive himself, he said, for needing nursed to the point of a girl's death. I had never seen him so fluent, so animated. If I had been told I was looking at his son, I would have believed it.

That night, after managing his house for a year, we consummated our marriage. He proved to be kind, and witty, and I slept for the first time thinking that my parents had chosen well. He asked where his men were; when I explained my ploy of the thing in the forest he fell silent and looked hard at me for a long time. I thought he was angry and pointed out that they had broken one woman's wrist and made free with the unmarried girls.

He said that he was not angry but admiring. He had not known I had such strategy in me. He said it was fortunate that I was young, though sad that he was old, because we could have made the place great for many generations. I felt that I was being tested, though I did not know for what. I said something about hoping he had many years left. He caught my arm tightly and asked if I meant it. I did and said so, and we slept.

His vigour lasted until the spring. The ice squeezed and popped, thawing just as he began to freeze up and petrify again. I had no more stuff for poultices and only a small jar of oil left. He slowed, turned sullen with pain, and became an old man again, clinging and wheedling. We argued and I realized that despite his age, I loved him and wanted no other husband. When I found that I was with child I was happy, but it was tempered with a fear that he would crumble and die, leaving me and the baby unprotected in a court guarded by wolves.

I dreamed fearful dreams. I had not told him about the child – nor have I ever asked if he knew. Honesty and happiness are weights on separate ends of a beam. Too much of one destroys the balance of a marriage.

I woke as he leaned over me. Despite the pain in his knotting joints, he was atop me on all fours like a dog. His face was tightly closed with an exquisite indrawing of something. He looked like a man in a rose garden whose every atom is given over to sucking in the perfume.

I felt faint, then fainter still, as if I was being diluted like wine in water. Some generative principle was being dragged out, disorganizing me. I raised a hand which no longer seemed my own, and his eyes opened. He rocked back on his heels, hectic spots in his cheeks, and I felt the pain begin.

The old women have assured me that phantom babes can appear and disappear, making a woman feel as if she carries a child when her womb is really empty. They said nothing about babes which had been alive until the life was sucked out of them. There is no point in asking.

The child's life, and the years it would have lived, have been added to my husband's, but I must find other breath to feed from or he will commit another wife to the pyre. To this end I sip from the girls around me, although they are beginning to draw away. It is never enough, and I am always hungry. They call me a lamia - one mother shouted it to my face when her baby stopped breathing on its third day. I couldn't answer because I likely would have sucked the child dry had the chance been there.

So I can scent Psyche's child and its stored breath, the pneuma which links its growing life to the world-soul, which I steal in sips like a boy at the wine jar. Heir to aer, I need its life. I am so hungry that I would risk the anger of a god for it.

Niobe

A bronze water jar and hanks of shorn hair lie on the steps of the house. No lamps burn outside the door or in the entrance way, and stepping over the threshold Psyche's sisters find more hair strewn. There are children's curls and short choppy wads of men's hair, grey and coarse. A thick fan shorn from a horse's mane is spread across the tiles like paint blown from a brush. The whole place is dark and cold and smells of tears and tallow.

Grief is expressed by leaving vital things undone: fire unburned; hair cut off; darkness gathering, movement unmade. *For you, we say, we will reel the universe back to the beginning and sit in the nothingness thinking that you brought order and meaning to it all.* We overstate the case to make our resurgence more incredible. *You see,* we tell ourselves, *you can come back from this.* The world has infinite beginnings. The lamp can be relit, hair regrown, death can be washed off like dust from the road.

The sisters toe the hanks of hair and look at each other, feeling horror at a grief they don't share. They have their stories ready. They concentrate on the cliff and the memory of the winds blowing around the valley when the Zephyr left them. *There was no sign of Psyche*, they prepare to say. *We don't know if she's been taken by a god or polished off by the vultures.*

The state of their mother stops them. Their father is out, dealing with his grief alone. Atthis sits on her bed, her eyes bulging and blood red, her hair in odd, uneven wads around her head. She looks like Medusa, fidgeting with a corner of Psyche's baby blanket. Afraid, they settle at her feet, smelling her rankness, listening to her muttering, struggling with an obedience that has destroyed her.

They turn her legs around onto the bed. Her eldest daughter holds her mother's head in her lap, stroking the ruined hair until she falls asleep. The other holds her mother's feet, and they look at each other along the length of Atthis' grief-stinking body, thinking that Psyche has caused another bloody mess and that they are sick to death of her dramas and glad that they are childless, if this is what motherhood brings you.

This is the basis of the love between parent and child – a mutual forgiveness for what you've done to each other.

Between her daughters' hands their mother dreams the dream of all parents: What is this life that I have magicked up within me? Through a rain-curtain of grief she dreams of weeping Niobe, whose boast of her many children brought her madness and grief.

Dreaming, Atthis stands on a riverbank holding a longnecked pot, the loutrophoros with which they washed Psyche in her sad nuptial bath, and which they put in her untenanted tomb. Atthis watches the river flow from spring to ocean, and knows the gods are trying to explain the nature of things to her. *You have pitched some tiny new consciousness into the river and commanded it to make sense of the flow, although neither the child nor the river is the same from moment to moment.*

You created in chaos, you brought forth in confusion. You hand on longing for stability to a new creature who perceives only the impermanence around and within it. And here is the condition which makes the pain exquisite: you have language to name it.

In her dream Psyche's mother wades into the water and tries to catch a ripple. She cannot even tell in which direction the river flows, or where it starts. All streams are like this. The grief that we experience once will, at least, never be repeated because it will not be the same grief and we will not be the same person.

It's not comforting: all you have is an endless variation of griefs, of confusion, of life. Grief is a return to the chaos from which the universe came. Grieving rituals sketch this chaos with household stuff. Grief, like extraordinary joy, is a glimpse of reality as humans see it.

In the background of her dream, Atthis senses a divine laughter. The gods do not grieve, nor do they see chaos, or indeed any categories at all. With no separation between things there is neither end nor beginning, just endless process. A river must be constantly changing to remain the river. The distinction between you and the world around you exists only in your head.

A mother remains a mother even when her children are dead. The constant change within defines her and that cycle of growing, bearing, and losing is part of the greater process of all things, all streams.

That's the gods' advice, anyway. Atthis turns it over in her dreaming mind and concludes that Psyche remains Psyche *because* she is now being ingested by worms.

In her dream Atthis smashes the long-necked pot and with a shard slashes at a firm sphere she knows somehow is Psyche's belly, determined that her daughter will not commit the same infamy of parenthood that now torments her.

Voluptas, unborn

In the life before life you listen to many voices.

I hang from my umbilicus like a bunch of grapes, looking at the clusters that will be my fingers, playing with the flippers of my soon-to-be-legs, pulling on the proto-penis that will not grow much more because I will be female. I drowse inside the glowing pomegranate of my mother and enjoy the little time I have left here, being alive but not yet human.

This is pleasure. I want to remain in this ruby snug forever. Hanging, globular, involved: being without the exhaustion of body; awareness without the burden of person.

I know when she is unhappy; the weather in here changes. I can hear them talking. It seems already as if life is many short bursts of wanting, then receiving, then rejoicing, then waning and souring. And yet they will call me Voluptas, Hedone, Bliss.

I know my father's voice. He speaks and the sky inside my mother darkens and she cries. My father never knew the tranquility of gestation, or he would not have begotten me. Barely in being, I already know that pain is caused when the gods try to compliment mankind – or when men construe their pain as divine interest.

When men imagine the divine, they inflate what they think is greatest in themselves. Cupid created me by concentrating that human trait which seems most miraculous to him. Not wisdom or courage – they have little of that between them – but bliss, the capacity to be satisfied. By nature, this is something a god cannot know.

Wishing to give my mother something that showed his awe of her humanity, Cupid summoned my soul from where we wait in the stygian darkness. I didn't mind it there. But the soul-drench of Lethe doesn't always do a thorough job, and streaks of past lives cling even as you're sent shooting off to the next one.

You might think that some leftover knowledge would be a benefit. It's not. What remains are the deepest stains, the scars and epiphanies that a quick scrub of death's forgetfulness can't wash off.

Unless you've had a remarkably fortunate life, dying young and gloriously, for instance, what sticks is the tiresomeness of being in a body. Lurking around the banks of the Lethe, some souls suggested that this might actually be living, and the walkers in the world above us were really the dead ones, their bodies their tombs.

The more I hear of my parents' voices, wrangling over the business of being, the easier it is to believe that I'm heading towards death, not birth. At this point, I give an irritable kick inside my mother. The voices in the outer world joyfully interpret this as my fierce desire to be out there and among them.

Embodied life, as you can see, is one misunderstanding after another.

Real pleasure is this guiltless drowse in the smallest antechamber of Hypnos' house. You'd be happy much more often without the chains of self-awareness which come from being in a body. In true pleasure you lose yourself. And since knowing yourself is the defining trait of humans, the more human you are, the less happy.

Cupid congratulates himself on submitting to the order of marriage, wife, home, and child. Psyche tries to discern some order in the husband she's never seen, and the fluttering of life within her. I feel myself being dragged into the same great ordering mill of matter. For the second (third, hundredth, who knows?) time I am moved into being by that force we perceive as order. It began as sperm and ovum united in defiance of randomness and kicked off the wearisome duplication into a zygote which, *sui generis*, is the opposite of chaos. Enmeshed in the net of biological order, I will experience life until the whole process climaxes and begins to retreat into death.

And they will call me Bliss.

This is the death of pleasure: you go through a narrow door, down a short tight passageway to a brightness and a world of expectation, and are born.

A God and a Teenage Girl

Cupid's head feels like a bag of wasps.

Psyche's stamina is incredible. He tries to remember whether there was a gradual build up to this shrillness, her astonishing skip from one topic to another, but it's no use – his brain is stuck in the sluggishness you feel after a truly terrible night's sleep when you've been woken every fifteen minutes by some violent noise, to the point where you fear you're going mad and you snap and cry and become tremulous over nothing, or maybe it's over something important but you can't remember what because your short term memory has died on its feet along with other capacities and you also realize that this is the result of dealing with the emotional cacophony of a teenage girl who was so beautiful that she rendered everyone dumbstruck and then proceeded to fill the silence all by herself until, presumably, they were so desperate for some peace and bloody quiet and an end to the questions – and, my god, *how* can so many things require comment or exclamation and at that *pitch*, it's the pitch that really does it, like a fly buzzing right at the entrance to your ear, so much that you *pray*, you – a god – pray for her to fall asleep and then you run out of this palace that you created for her, into the silent garden and you plead tearfully for a silent world, so hard that you too fall asleep in the soft grass and sleep like the dead until you wake and it's night again and by some appalling turn you're back in the bedroom and she's already talking without even needing a conversation partner because she just wants to offload her *feelings* onto you, about how she's bored and lonely and has no one to talk to and, oh, look, the baby's kicking, give me your hand, there, can you feel it, I'm sure it's a boy because he kicks so strongly and if it's a boy he'll look like you and *then* I'll know what you look like even though it's ridiculous for a woman not to know her husband's face but actually it reminds me of a childhood friend of my mother's who had this eye problem and never knew what anyone looked like because all she could see straight in front of her was a black circle and she'll go on about this parental acquaintance for so long that your ears start to buzz and you'll wonder if there's an aural equivalent of this macula that she's describing, just something that immediately occludes any really insistently present noise, but despite your divine powers you cannot change so much as one decibel of your beloved and so once again you're reduced to fleeing your own house and going to Olympus, to that divine assembly space where couches are laid out and a perpetual dinner party is always going on except now, because the whole place is empty but for a couple of minor deities pushing a broom about and minding their own business, and they don't even seem to hear her infernal chatter, which has chased you up Olympus like a swarm of bees and brings you to your knees begging for Ares or Artemis or any other armed power who'll help you shut her up, even your mother, who now sits down before you on one of the sofas and coolly regards you, square-mouthed and sniveling like a baby because you're knackered, nerves shredded like Odysseus' travelling cloak, heartily sick of matchless Psyche and heartily sorry that you didn't obey your mother's orders to the letter and make her fall in love with the Malum, that wicked thing through which Psyche would be punished, which goddess now looks at you stonily and says she's extremely glad to hear that you're sorry, but that you both have an appropriate punishment, and that marriage is for life and it'll serve you right, so suck it up, go home to the girl you preferred to your own mother, and get yourself a garden shed and a lawnmower and look forward to being respectably widowed, which is how most of mankind deals with the long aftermath of your arrows, and when I'm satisfied that you'll never again disobey me, then you'll get your heaven of peace and quiet.

Nostos

The girl staggered into the little market-place around midday as the stall holders were pulling canvas covers over the goods and getting ready for an afternoon snooze in the shade of their barrows. The country was too small for anyone to be a stranger, and there were only two ways for strangers to come – over the mountains or by the port. She had arrived by neither route, nor could anyone get a word out of her to explain her sudden appearance. Then she fainted.

Spectrally thin, her hair fell below her knees in the manner of a corpse, in whom hair and nails continue to grow when the rest of the body has begun to rot. When sponged clean of road dust and grass stains from a long and haphazard journey, her face was undeniably beautiful. Someone, recalling an old rumour about the king's missing youngest child, thought to call for the royal nurse. It was she who, on turning the girl over, found the small strawberry birthmark at the top of a high, curved left buttock, showing that Psyche had finally returned home.

When she woke, still dazed and with no clear memory of entering the little agora, Psyche was translated to her parents' house and laid in the bed she had shared with her sisters decades before. Letters were sent to the sisters, now mothers many times over, saying only, 'She has returned.' In their own countries they read this with untroubled brows and then went back to their own lives.

Psyche slept for many days, her presence seeping into the house like a draught whose source can never quite be found. Separately, her parents came to gaze on her, wondering where she had been and how the years could have left her barely aged. They did not know how to respond to this surprising turn of events.

Psyche may have returned home, but other abducted girls – Persephone, and Europa, and Semele, probably even Helen – do not. There is no homecoming for women. There is only the familiar and repeated story of the abducted girl, the stories of a man and a dark place where she is controlled absolutely, her reappearance years later with the signs of pregnancy and motherhood, and her family's mixed reaction to this sudden, and not always welcome, reappearance. Girls going missing is in the blood of the human species.

Occasionally she opened her eyes and looked up at them without seeing, and they wondered how they could feel so little for their own child, who was now a stranger to them. They discussed the day she vanished in the mountains in the middle of a noisy family picnic. Neither had a clear recollection of the day any more, nor did their few memories agree with each other. She had gone, they had torn the mountains, their own city, and then neighbouring cities apart in search of her. Her mother, who kept the rites of Dionysus and led the maenads in revel, was accused of killing her daughter in an unseasonal frenzy, and her husband of covering it up. Their inability to cry, in the face of what became malicious scrutiny, endeared them to no one.

Time passed and gossip coagulated into two stories about Psyche's disappearance: the public story of the beautiful child who had vanished at the hands of her parents, and the private story in her parents' heads of a sunny day, a ball game, of packing up baskets and the first blue fingers of evening in the sky and the discovery that she was simply gone.

Now, they looked at the girl in the bed and found no echo of themselves in her long limbs, her straight nose and noble jaw, not even in the signs – undeniable, said the physician and two midwives – that she had known the pains of childbirth. She was simply a mystery into which they had not been inducted, nor did they want to be.

After two days she woke in the night and called for her nurse, now quite decrepit, who came to her bedside and took her hand. Psyche poured out a story about a great house, a decades-long darkness broken sometimes by a man who brought food and candlelight and the burning oil of his desire. Never once did she lay eyes on him, though he got children by her. Nor did he treat her badly, though he infected her with a desire which burned through her, melting the fat from her bones, making her skeletal, insatiable, ageless.

At some point she woke from the fever-dream of desire. She went to the unlocked door and stood outside the house, which she thought looked golden in the moonlight. She could give no account of the territory where she had been held, or even measure accurately the time that she had been away. She understood that it was long, because her parents were so aged. It did not trouble her. Nothing troubled her any more. She was beyond desiring vengeance and returned to bed.

In the morning, her parents came to her bedside resolved on action. Her mother embraced the nurse, who had fallen asleep holding the girl's hand. Her father shook Psyche's frail shoulder, gently, then harder, until it was evident that she had disburdened herself of her story, and her life with it. He slid the knife back into his sleeve and called for women to wash and shroud her.

Twice-buried, Psyche's homecoming was not made public. No funeral dirge was played over her tomb, which her parents took care to seal with lead.

Silphium

Behind the pastos, they are all tangled together on the bed: Cupid, crooning like a raven over Psyche's belly; Psyche holding the chaos of life within her like a bucket of sea water; thoughts of her sisters' malice and the memory of their childhood sweetness; the burning coal of her curiosity, and all of this wrapped up in the golden cord of life, which continues like a joke that has gone on too long.

In the morning, she goes into the garden and cuts a long stalk of silphium, makes a tea of its leaves, and jettisons the dubious gift of Cupid's child. When it comes, she inspects the blood and marvels that so much anguish begins in this thick black pool where clots and fantasies, gods and tissue are indifferently mixed.

Her faceless husband is furious. In the dark he sounds checkmated. She stands by the window so that he can see the bulky mess of cloths soaking up the remnants of their child. Now that she is so unattractive, she thinks, he will listen.

He demands explanations. Why did she do it? Doesn't she value the gift of life? What would become of mankind if they all did this?

'Imagine our child,' she says, 'suffering as I am now suffering. Imagine it, burning though the days of its life – a life it knows will be short and lived with one eye on the end – in a fury of desire, of curiosity, of rejoicing and sorrow. Imagine this child, exhausted by even the quietest life, coming to us and saying, *Why did you create me? What could we possibly say that does not begin with I wanted?*'

Cupid is glad of the darkness, which hides his shame and anger. What about the joys of life, he asks. What if the child is as beautiful as you, invulnerable to harm, what if he knows only ecstasy through his life, which will be eternal.

He hears the smile in her voice as she easily refutes him.

She laughs. 'If you can offer all this, why add consciousness? Make him a star immediately; save him the knowledge of time, of otherness, of watching his own friends wither and die. Gods and lovers talk lightly of the joys of human life, but name one person who does not overstate the case. It's lopsided any way you look at it. If he is born, he will suffer. That is inevitable, and a harm. He may also rejoice, but this is uncertain, although it could be counted a good. If he is not born, he will not suffer, and this is certainly a good. He will also escape those uncertain joys. That cannot be counted a harm because he does not yet exist – and how can you harm something which has no being? In the two pans of this scale, the heavier weight lies in the pan of not-being.'

For once, Cupid feels his fire gutter and threaten to go out. He imagines what the world would be if Psyche's dangerous idea took hold. Remote and terrifying humans, thanking the gods for nothing, cursing them as bringers of another burden. Eventually, a quiet earth, empty but for animals whose desire to mate and multiply is untainted by self-consciousness.

There is nothing more to say. In the morning they part; Psyche to her own unpeopled future, where she waits peacefully for her end, content that she has not added her womb to the catalogue of ships carrying new people to new and bloody futures. Cupid, burned by this moment of clarity, departs his golden palace, but not without first cursing the silphium, which never grows again.

Wish

Psyche would, she says, rather die a hundred deaths than allow herself to be tricked into looking on her husband's face. In the divine mind where many possible worlds exist, Cupid watches her die these hundred deaths.

In her first death Psyche blinds herself, like Oedipus, from horror at her own oath-breaking. Cupid watches her from the shadows and it is impossible to say whether he approves, shares her horror, or is simply impassive. The gods feel no horror, just as they feel no joy.

It is not clear whether he returns her to life, or her own preference for ninety-nine more deaths does. Either way she suffers the agonies of dying once, and then in a flicker returns to life, ready to die again. And again. Each time is as dreadful as the first, because each time seems like the only death – death would, after all, be meaningless if we did it repeatedly. With each death Psyche looks annihilation in the face and, with the madness of a zealot, clings to the idea that this is a kind of freedom. She is too taken up with dying to realize that in facing death she has seen something important about Cupid. Death and love are different expressions of the immensity in which we lose and find ourselves.

Each time he resurrects her, he asks whether she would still rather die a hundred times than break her promise not to look at his face. Each time he is amazed at her unwavering resolution. She holds on so hard to an idea of herself that she cannot see its pointlessness. A hundred deaths is meaningless. One death is enough.

He wakes her from a sound and happy sleep and hands her a knife. *Your wrists*, he says. Exhausted, she botches it and he must finish the job. It takes her over an hour to bleed to death, weeping and white, lying in the bed she will never leave.

Immediately she is resurrected, with all the scars of her suicide but none of the memory. This time there is a preparation of hemlock by the bed. *Drink*, he says. *It is the only way to stop yourself seeking the sight of my face.* The same arguments, the same limpet-fast clinging to life, the same capitulation.

Resurrected a hundred times, each time she bears all the marks and the exhaustion of the backlog of deaths she has suffered. At her hundredth death he reveals to her – now ruined by scars, shadows, poison-blotches, crooked, bald, and toothless – what has passed. She cannot take it all in. Now he readies her for the last of it. *Tell me*, he says, *tell me that you would rather die a hundred times than look on my face. And when you say it, know that human deaths are meaningless to someone who cannot die. It is like watching a fish swim, a bird fly, any creature performing that task which alone constitutes its nature. Tell me that you prefer a hundred deaths over doing what is in your nature.*

Wrecked, Psyche stares at the outline in the darkness of the man who has taken her beauty, her baby, her life, and now demands her dignity. She feels an unutterable happiness at this lapidary demand. *God exists*, she thinks. *Such extremity, such insistence on my own free will can only be divine.*

He has presented her with a hopeless choice so that she will realize that her situation is untenable. Seeing her happiness, he sighs. At this rate, he thinks, he will never be known.

Inventions

'Remind me what your husband does, again?'

Her sisters will never meet him – nor, Psyche thinks, will she. In drawing these verbal portraits she's telling her sisters something more important: Fate has forced her to invent a life, so she will fill the husband-shaped gap with whatever she wants. She uses stories, memories, imaginary people, this house of desire and illusions to patch up the parts where life has given her no foothold. Beware people whom you have cast off; they are anchored to no single story.

He's a merchant, she says. Import/export. Large sums. Foreign travel. He's middle-aged, grey just touching his temples. She hears a suppressed snigger and realizes that he is listening. *Fine*, she thinks grimly. *If I am just a playing piece in your absurd fantasy, you're one in mine.*

Confusion flickers across her sisters' faces. This is the other side of the golden house, the treasure, the baby, she wants to say. Fantasies, fictions, gaps filled with your own invention – or unfilled. This is the life of the poets: beautiful, chimerical, diaphanous, thin, exhausting.

Knowing that Psyche is lying to them, her sisters decide to be outraged. Only suspicious people invent stories, they decide, and only the wicked invent good stories. Making things up is a kind of arrogance because it suggests that reality is unsatisfactory. It's antisocial to go about making up things. It defies the power of the group, that sharp shared plane which brings everyone down to a common level. To her sisters, invention is solitary and thus pointless. So either Psyche is telling lies for the fun of it, or she's lying from the shame of not knowing what her own husband looks like. If it's the former, she is wicked. If the latter, she's stupid and wicked. In their outrage they decide he must be a god. And if he's a god, Psyche's carrying a divine child.

If she's the mother of a divine child, I will hang myself, says the elder sister, who knows there is no chance she'll be reminded of this promise.

The Thracian women

Her sisters decide to wait until Psyche is delivered of the child, and when he is born his utter helplessness makes them wait a little longer before they orphan him. It is a full ten years, as long as a war, before they can bring themselves to the task.

Throughout this time Psyche has stuck to her agreement. The boy, Xenos, shows the signs of divinity, and she still has no more notion of his father's face than a fish of the sky. It has sent her mad: daily she looks at the stranger slowly emerging from her son's face and fears that when the boy is on the brink of manhood she will fall in love with him as the visible face of his invisible father. A maelstrom of fear and longing consumes her and she wanders the halls, a prisoner of two captors now, talking to herself and laughing.

Afraid that she will speak love-words to her son, she cuts out her tongue. Her husband fills the space with his own. At last, her sisters can bear it no longer.

'Listen,' they tell her, 'he has ruined you and us too. When we first came here we were jealous of your wealth, jealous of your child, jealous of the free hand with which you feasted us, bathed us, gifted treasures from these trashy piles of gold. We went away planning to bring you down – you, our little sister!

'We lied to our parents, our husbands, to you. We have become the worst versions of ourselves. And as for you – we do worse than fear for you now; we pity you, because you are so pathetic a spectacle that Prometheus wouldn't steal an olive for you, let alone fire. What's next? Pushing a cart with all your worldly goods? Going through middens? You can't even answer because you tossed away your own tongue. Our dignity is like a storm-shredded sail. It demands vengeance.'

The first Cupid knows of it is the shadow of a spindly phallus bobbing over him as he sleeps. He feels a sharp smack as it hits him – not a phallus at all but a thyrsus, ivy-wound, pine-tipped and painful.

Then they are upon him, howling and glutted with chaos. They tear apart his son, lest he repeat his father's tyranny.

Laughing, Cupid leaps away and is pursued through his own halls, slipping on the skid-trails of blood from poor, dismembered Xenos. Trailing wine-fumes and the smell of pitch the three sisters close on him. Naked and entwined with Cupid, they tear him arm from torso, leg from pelvis, wrenching the head free from the well-built archer's body which is now just an octopus trailing tendons and flanks of gore.

They are so covered in blood that each does not know which sister she is, or if they are three women at all and not one, smashing the mirror which has long been held before her face.

They place a wolf cub in Psyche's arms.

They tear through the garden, the glade, the forest, and come eventually to the cliff where they bay like wolves. Dwindling, collapsing, they sleep sprawled out on the rocks and the moon stands stern guard over them.

In the dark the dismembered parts of Cupid slowly merge together again, repooling like mercury. Reunited, Cupid sits up, laughing and rubbing his shoulder. In the morning he will answer his mother's summons to avenge her injured prerogatives, usurped by a girl called Psyche, who now sleeps in her parents' home between her loving, watchful sisters.

Categories

The problem of her husband's identity is really a problem about Psyche's capacity to know something. When we deny someone knowledge, we deny them the exercise of their ability to know something. Behind her husband's demand that she does not look upon his face, Psyche recognizes a fear of being known.

Here is what she can say of him after their months together. This darkness to which she is married has the arms and belly of an archer. His thighs are full and strong from running, but towards what? Away from what? The embodied night which climbs between her sheets has curls and a strong brow ridge. Although his skin is smooth and his cheek bare beneath her fingers, only an old man could lie so still when she touches him.

She never hears him approach, but there is a brightening of the air, heralding an absolute stillness, as of the moment before rain. She knows that he is a god the same way that we know it is about to snow.

She considers what else this male substance possesses. What is his quantity – how much is he? All she has are the domestic measurements that are the mathematics of love. She estimates that, with his head against the bedhead, he is one handspan shorter than the bed is long.

Of his qualities she has no idea. Able to love. Able to tell that it is night and time to be with her. Able to know from an impossible distance, what her sisters say and think. Of his capacity for relationships she has proof of only two: herself, and a breath of wind. Perhaps also the child that grows within her. Two thirds of his friends, then, are not fully human.

Where is he? In her darkened bedroom, if he is anywhere. Perhaps the bedroom is the substance and he is the accident, a quality of the room. Can he exist in any other place, and at any other time than night?

Of his extension in space she is more certain, since they have tried every plane and vertex in the room against their paired curves and solids.

Of the last categories, she is almost afraid. What does he have? What does he do? What, in the whole earth, experiences him? What if the answer to all three questions is her?

After carefully considering what can be said about her husband, Psyche decides that his essential nature is informed by desire, and that the end towards which his actions move him is fulfilment. Knowing that every material thing is a shadow of a higher entity Psyche decides to make a pilgrimage to the shrine of Eros at Thespiae, to ask Cupid for a sight of this husband who is a collection of accidents waiting to happen.

Pephuke

Throughout all the deceptions and metamorphoses, the gods have always chosen when the mask is dropped.

Leda, bleeding and uncertain about exactly what has just happened with the swan, watches it walk away. In the distance it becomes a man who moves with the same swan-massy, arrogant gait.

Danae, drowsing in the oven of her bronze tower, thinks the shower of gold was a figment of the mid-afternoon torpor, until the last flecks cohere into a human foot, leaping away into the cerulean sea.

Demeter, exhausted from searching for Persephone, turns herself into a mare to graze quietly among the Arcadian herd. Covered by a black stallion, she experiences some surprise when the shining horse becomes Poseidon, withdrawing sleazily back to the sea in his own form.

The gods lie around the sofas of Olympus and justify their deceptions. *It's all the same substance: horse and sea; man and swan; gold and god. If you can't see past the surperfice you deserve to be tricked.*

Or again, *It's only names. Call it the Dioscuri, St Elmo's fire, cloud. It makes no difference to the thing itself. This is evidence of human stupidity, to worship the names.*

Or *We show people the illusions they entertain about themselves. If you want to call your inconvenient pregnancy the work of a shower of gold, that's up to you.*

Their divine wives look away, disgusted, but they do not stop the gods.

Until a mortal does the unmasking. Pretty Iris, who danced everywhere and saw everything, Cupid's friend and close confidant – so much that it was whispered, wrongly, that she was his mother. An old man, hearing his neighbor tell a child that the bow in the sky was the goddess' girdle, said *Rubbish. What you call Iris is by nature just coloured cloud.*

Hearing this, Iris turns to Cupid for reassurance, but already she is transparent. What were once eyes, a smile, the shape of his fleet-footed friend, Iris of the pretty gown, is now just a play of elements he cannot access. His eyes blur with tears. Why are things never revealed the other way around – a coloured cloud is really a goddess? How long will it be before a different world recognizes again the godhead in rain-spheres struck by pure light?

It causes him agony to think that Iris knew herself to be an illusion in her last moments.

Now, hiding in the shadows of his own house while Psyche leads her sisters around, Cupid hears the powerful word spoken again. *Pephuke.* The real nature of a thing. They tell her that the bulky length she has slept beside for months, which has fathered her child and taught her desire is really a snake. Her sisters say that Cupid is really a snake because they know that these things – desire, dilation, consumption - are what women fear most.

Psyche sees that it fits. His voraciousness, his insinuation into her every crevice, the fury of his heat, the desire which is poison. It is like a magic knot; the spell loops once, then back upon itself, and is cast.

Pephuke. The powerful word is spoken. Cupid knows himself for what he is. His pupils narrow; his arms weld themselves to his sides; the world becomes smell and vibration. Before his snaky brain overwhelms him he sees that Psyche's sisters, whom he had called liars and tormentors, are his liberators.

The illusion dies, Iris dies, look for your gods.

Consumption

Much later, when she has been cast out to wander the world, Psyche will recall this afternoon and formulate three axioms about storytelling. One is that stories are most convincing when told at the right time to the right person. Like a ball hitting a bat at the optimum point, every listener has a moment in which they are maximally receptive.

The second axiom is that the person who has told you happy stories, stories which hearten, encourage, beguile you, is precisely the person who will one day tell you a story which poisons.

So her sisters, tellers of those thrilling stories of ghosts, nymphs, family infidelities, the vast invisible substructure of girls' hopes, arrive to poison Psyche with a story. Of course they hit the sweet spot – since her child began to thrash about like an elver inside her, she has been wide open to any story, except her husband's.

The best lies are told in daylight, without preamble. Her sisters are talking even before the zephyr has put them down: *You're not going to believe this…*

You know you said he was smooth and muscular, and so very tall?

That you could feel his muscles sliding under his skin?

That his tongue…well, you know what you said about his tongue?

How do we tell you this…you'll hate us. But we must – for the baby's sake. He's a snake. It's not a man at all.

Yes, like Typhoön.

Come on – you know he's a god. You've always *known. And don't you feel it, twisting and flipping around inside you, curled around your very guts, just like a snake?*

It's not just us – there are farmers around here – yes, truly, but has he ever let you see them? They won't come near this place. They call it the Serpent Palace. They've seen him, gliding home at night through the fields, swimming in the river, sleeping in the sun fat with a bullock. He is going to fatten you with the child and then eat you.

The third axiom is that lies are simply stories in which the frame is invisible.

Swelling painfully with this foreign object which has started like a cyst, it all rings horribly true to Psyche. The inner zoetrope which runs together all the insinuations asks, *Can I* see *this happening?* And inside Psyche's head a voice says, *Yes, I can see him consuming me.*

Oeconomia

Women tell the worst stories to women.

Years later, when Odysseus and Penelope are frail, Nausicaa's daughter comes to Ithaca as a match for Telemachus. From her new daughter-in-law Penelope hears the missing part of her husband's wanderings.

Out of all the monsters, the trials and temptations, Nausicaa, whom Odysseus first sees with her arms full of washing, is the one thing he never mentioned to Penelope. As Nausicaa's daughter relates how her mother met Odysseus, Penelope stares into the fire and keeps a well-practiced smile on her face as many small absences – of mind, of affection, of hope – in the years since Odysseus came home fall into place.

Listening to the girl's story, Penelope pictures it: Odysseus, his very clothes torn off by the sea, climbing onto the dunes naked and exhausted from the ocean. The gadfly wind, always present and always blowing him off course, pummels his sun-scorched shoulders. He wakes and stands, dizzy and disbelieving, at the flock of girls naked and shining pink as the lips of nautilus shells, throwing a ball among the flapping linen. The whole picture blurs in his drowned head and he confuses them with the ravenous gulls. Another island, another illusion, more women. His chin begins to quiver as tears of exhaustion fall. He drops to his knees. He blocks the sun. A man-shaped shadow slants across the white sheets. The girls turn, scream, scatter. Only Nausicaa is left.

On his knees in the dune Odysseus is level with Nausicaa's eyes. And this is the moment that troubles Penelope. It lies between her and Odysseus in the great living olive-tree bed that symbolizes his ingenuity and which solved the question of his identity. Penelope congratulated herself for asking the one question that only her husband could have answered. Now it torments her. To everyone else it showed her wit, but it also showed Odysseus that she did not recognize him. She did not know the man for whom she had waited those many long years. Whereas Nausicaa recognized him instantly as her natural other half.

Who knows what Odysseus and Nausicaa said to each other in the dunes, alone and naked like another Deucalion and Pyrrha? Her daughter-in-law's voice fades into the background and Penelope thinks about Nausicaa, the teenage princess who did not flee this naked, salt-encrusted stranger, or make threats or pleas, but immediately devised a plan to gain him sanctuary and patronage. Nausicaa received him like a queen, because even in the middle of the weekly laundry some part of her is always waiting and planning, and is never caught by surprise when her missing half turns up out of nowhere.

She gives him some of the laundry to wear. Before her friends have even come creeping back from their hiding places she has explained that her mother is the real brain of their island kingdom.

Suddenly Penelope feels less clever. She offers to comb her daughter-in-law's hair. They both know that this will save her from looking at the girl's face.

Her new daughter does not mention that Nausicaa begged her parents for the stranger's hand. Perhaps her mother did not tell her this part but Penelope feels it out anyway, like a lump in the bedsheets of the story.

She tries to get a fix on what troubles her most. Odysseus did not sleep with Nausicaa. Other women pulled him from the sea and tried to keep him for themselves. He left them all, she reminds herself, to return to Ithaca and to me.

Was he in love with Nausicaa? Penelope knows the difference between *himeros*, the spell-binding attraction that someone can exercise upon you, and *pothos*, the longing for something dearest to your heart. She and Telemachus and their home were the *pothos* which drove Odysseus back to Ithaca.

She decides that what troubles her is that Odysseus did not tell her this story. It has filtered into the separate world of women's stories. Like groundwater, silent and pervasive, the stories of women are different to the big bluster of mythos, which Telemachus once reminded his mother was a man's business.

Penelope knows that the mythos of men directs your works and days but the stories of women colour your dreams and nightmares. Men build back doors and loopholes into their stories, which allow heroes to be cowardly, childish, implacable, and wicked. Women's stories are simple and uncompromising: *This is life. You will suffer. You will find out why too late. The jar of your thoughts is the only thing you truly own. If you want to be respected, bear children. If you want to be happy, don't.* She does not like the thought of Odysseus and Nausicaa bottled up together inside the jar of women's stories.

But what can she do? She keeps combing the girl's hair, now glossier than a brood mare's, and listens as Nausicaa's daughter talks on. There are two stories, Penelope sees now, and at the heart of both is a profound absence. Faithful Penelope is absent from the story of Odysseus and Nausicaa. And Nausicaa, the burner of ships and hander-out of laundry to castaways, is absent from Odysseus' story to his wife. It is as though Nausicaa and Penelope cannot both exist in the same space. And in both stories, Penelope thinks, is the problem of recognition: of Odysseus by a woman, and of what will benefit him by Odysseus himself. She may have been immortalized in the swaggering yarns of men, but Penelope will always feel that she has failed.

Although she keeps combing, Penelope feels tears start in her eyes. When he returned, a caution born of years of strength and stratagem made her miss the moment. She mistook Odysseus for another vagabond. The picture torments her: Odysseus on the dunes, Nausicaa taking in the sight of him and knowing without words that he is her natural partner. Men will not see this; women will not see anything but this.

Winding up, Telemachus' new wife says that none of it matters because she's here now, isn't she? And Telemachus is wonderful, beautiful, the best husband ever.

Both women know that the real wedding gift which Nausicaa's daughter has brought to Ithaca is the story that Odysseus kept from Penelope. A story that secures the girl's future, and that of her children.

There is a sound and they see Odysseus in the doorway, the puppy Hector at his heels. Penelope knows there is no point wondering how long he was there, or how much he heard. That is the nature of marriage to this complicated man, full of secrets and wiles, most of which he has made necessary himself. And Odysseus knows that the economy of women's stories is about establishing value, like appraising a necklace. The stories say, 'You're worth this much, and I this much'.

He shepherds his wife to bed, to dream or not, and reminds himself to forbid women's stories in his home.

Future

The problems of bringing a child into the world will never change.

I was coming back from work just on dawn, my head full of stray tag lines from the Rage of Gaia campaign. One of the pumps had failed; the whole southern half of the city was swimming.

Her face was tilted up at me from the klong silt, full of dirt and night garbage. She had the vertical pupils of a CRISPer from Pagasan or Itu Aba. A round face with apple cheeks and a mouth like a bao. She was starving. I was starving.

She made a swallowing noise, like a cry, and held out a hand.

*

Her forked tongue had been removed, so I filled her mouth with mine.

This was desire; feeding on the meat of each other.

Forty square feet for us both, for months on end. Her growing belly did all the talking for her. The space shouted with the baby.

*

I was working for the new population control campaign: Back to 8 Billion. We took a carrot and stick approach: the carrot was protection against the swarms of illegals and CRISPers lapping at our borders with their ophid eyes and insatiable wombs. We used old footage of a beautiful Pagasan girl, her face slightly averted, hauling herself from a trafficker's Coandă near the city barriers. Dripping wet, we thought her sinuous shape would antagonize women and agitate men. She turned, her pupils opening like a flower, and lunged to feed on her rescuer.

The stick was future-eating. Cannibal parents; post-partum mothers snacking on the jellied softness of their newborns. The government made a new law. The last human taboo - consuming your own child - became the penalty for unregistered breeding.

We broadcast infrasound narremes near food outlets. This was the story; desire, dilation, consumption. I could not shake the feeling that it was a twice-told tale.

She stayed a prisoner in our forty square feet of panic and inertia, and swelled.

*

Briefly she covered my face with her hands and then took them away, cupped, as if holding an imprint of my face. She gestured to the world outside the window and showed me her cupped hands high, low, here, there, against the bright square of the glass. *Faces*, her hands said. *I want to see faces out there.* She drew a rectangle around herself in the air. A coffin? No, alone. Isolated. Without seeing others she was alone. She put my hand over her eyes. *You are making me blind.*

What else could I do? She was illegal. Our child was illegal. I shut her in even more tightly.

*

She fought me off, ran out. I imagined her standing on the sidewalk with the people pouring around her, drinking in the faces in the neon and drizzle, until her belly drew attention. By the time I reached the street she had been picked up. I saw the tail-lights of a police zephyr flash once, then vanish in the mist.

*

I sat by the window and waited for them to come. I told myself the story we had lived: saving, imprisoning, coupling, generating, breaking, burning. It seemed familiar, but I have told so many stories that I cannot remember where I first heard it.

*

And now the beaker, with its thick, syrupy contents. They have a way of preparing it: dried and then ground down to rough granules. Not fine enough to dissolve entirely though. Pinky-gray granules drift in the viscose stuff, reminding you of what it was.

You can swallow it, relentlessly visible in your glass box to the crowd below. Like a sandworm, you move along eating and excreting as you go. Moving in a circle, eating your own offspring. A father consuming his children, a snake-woman, a flooded world – the same things happened at the beginning of time.

Or you can not swallow it. If you throw the beaker against the walls you will have to sit there with it, the ash of your child, smeared over the glass walls of this prison that you will never leave.

.

Masque

DRAMATIS PERSONAE:
KOUROS (a young man)
PSYCHE
CUPID

The portico of Cupid's house, with stairs before a vast pair of doors. The doors are carved with images of the disasters caused by Desire. In the distance, drawing nearer, is the sound of hooves, and a high-pitched whistling, as of wheels at speed. Up to these doors comes a young man, a kouros. He has coconut-halves tied around his knees so that when he runs it sounds like horses galloping. The whistling sound comes from a pipe, which he is blowing.

He stops at the steps and shouts out.

KOUROS: Helllooooo! Anyone home?

There is a prolonged pause, where he examines the doors. Then one door is opened, minimally, and Psyche sticks her head out.

PSYCHE: Oh! I thought I heard something. Horses or…

KOUROS: [*making the coconuts clop together*] Just me, a poor traveler, a seeker on the road of truth, hungry and thirsty.

PSYCHE: [*Coming all the way out so that we can see that she is vastly pregnant.*] We don't get many of those. Actually, you're the first person I've seen for months. Let me get you something to eat.

The Kouros sweeps a courtly bow and makes to follow her into the house. Psyche turns to prevent him.

Umm…we're a rather unusual household. Servants not fit to be seen and so forth. Would you mind eating out here?

KOUROS: No, not at all.

He sits down, while Psyche vanishes behind the doors. There is the sound of banging and clattering, and coins and metal trinkets scattering across the floor.

PSYCHE: [*Shouting from behind the door*] Have you come far?

KOUROS: [*grandly*] From the very gates to the roads of Night and Day, with the Daughters of the Sun attending me. They cunningly convinced Justice herself to open the gates and admit me to the Road of Truth.

Psyche emerges with a tray of food, and a pitcher and tumbler. All the dishes and the tray are made of gleaming gold.

Good lord. Are those gold dishes? Have I stumbled on a royal summer retreat?

PSYCHE: They were all I could find. They're much too heavy, but they're to my husband's taste. You were saying that Justice gave you directions?

KOUROS: [*Eating and pouring some wine*] Yes, she did. So what does he do, your husband?

PSYCHE: He's out. A lot.

KOUROS: Maybe I'll run into him. What does he look like?

PSYCHE: He's tall, I think. And his hair smells of cinnamon. And he does archery in his spare time, so his shoulders are very strong. And once, when he was a child, he had a fight with another boy over knucklebones, and he has a very tiny scar on his left inner thigh.

KOUROS: I don't think I'll be in a position to know him from any of that. Unless we end up snuggling, for some reason. I rather meant his face. What does he look like facially?

PSYCHE: I'm not much help there. I'm not really of a descriptive turn. Anyway, I see him so rarely that sometimes I wonder if he exists at all.

KOUROS: [*Eyeing her bump, which kicks occasionally*] Well, if he didn't it might be necessary to invent him. And pretty quickly, too.

PSYCHE: [*Beginning to cry, hopelessly*] Don't even talk about it. You could say he's just accidents waiting to happen. [*Sniffling, pulling herself together*] That's a joke. [*There is a silence*] Take your time.

KOUROS: Forgive my impertinence, but you seem unhappy. Is there anything I can do? Is it your household? Your husband?

PSYCHE: He hides himself from me. He won't let me see him, even though I run his household and carry his child. He doesn't live like me, like any mortal.

KOUROS: But this is the heart of most problems – does anyone exist *in the same way* as anyone else? Why do we even worry about the *way* that someone exists: how quickly they work, or how long their hair is, or what their face is like when we complain to them? We're all here, we all have Being, in one way or another.

PSYCHE: [*Beginning to snivel again*] And that'd be enough for you, would it?

KOUROS: 'Enough' suggests that you're measuring their being against some fixity, like a price. It's not for you to measure Being, which is immeasurable. Just let it go and contemplate the fact that you both *are*.

PSYCHE: You cannot possibly be married. Look, if that's true, then I have as much Being as a god. And if I had as much being as a god, why would I need anyone else, even another god?

KOUROS: You *don't* need anyone else. You *are*. They are. On a level which precedes thought and existence, you're both the same.

PSYCHE: But I need to know what he looks like! I want to know!

KOUROS: That's different. You're just fussing about accidents. Even your ignorance has being.

PSYCHE: I can see why philosophers rarely marry.

KOUROS: Being isn't the same as existence. Being is a precursor to existence. Existence simply describes the *way* that you be. As a god, for instance. Or as a woman. Or an unborn. Or a story about them.
There is a long pause in which Psyche twists and turns and is evidently trying to make up her mind whether or not to tell the Kouros something.

PSYCHE: I wasn't joking when I said that I wonder if he exists at all. It terrifies me. My sisters tell me that he's a huge snake, fattening me and my child to eat. Because they don't know what he is. And they know that *I don't know* – me, his wife! There's this huge gap about him, and in it anyone can fill in their worst imaginings. I fear the nothingness of it. What I really fear…what I really fear is that there's nothing there. That my husband has no Being.

KOUROS: That's impossible. It's impossible even to think or say it; we're built only to deal with what is. And everything *is*, everything has Being. You may not be thrilled about the *way* it has Being, but it's definitely there in one way or another.

PSYCHE: But if there *is* no Nothing, that's the same as saying Nothing is a Something. And everything has an opposite, so how can the opposite of Something be itself?

KOUROS: Who says everything has an opposite? That's just a little structure of thinking that your brain has got into. And the language you use to express it is exactly the same – they're all just routines for tidying what our senses tell us into a neat picture of the world. Really, though, they're very unhelpful. They're just a reason for us to be unhappy about the way something is. We do love the idea of opposites: human and divine, light and dark, same and different, male and female…

PSYCHE: Visible and invisible….

KOUROS: Exactly. Visibility is just an accident; it's not essential to the being of anything except perhaps a painting. And some things manage very well without. What would the wind look like, if we could see it?

PSYCHE: What about a husband – what if you couldn't see him?

KOUROS: Does it affect his being your husband? What would happen if you went blind – would *your* blindness make him less of a husband? Remember what I said about wind. That applies to husbands too.

PSYCHE: What about wind?

KOUROS: If it's there, particularly in a husband, it's better not to see it.

PSYCHE: [*Laughing and pointing at his coconut shells*] But wouldn't you rather have horses that exist?

KOUROS: Why? I mean, physical horses are grumpy, expensive, and inconvenient. This way I have the effect of horses, but none of the cost. They have being, but the manner of their existence is different from a horse of flesh and blood. It's only people who believe that this is better. In fact, all states have their benefits. Come and I'll show you.

[*He gets up and clops to the front of the steps, holds out a hand and toots his pipe.*] Step up on my chariot, which has being but a less cumbersome

137

manner of existence than some hotrod that will break my neck. Come up!

PSYCHE: [*Stands up and waddles down the stairs*] What do I do?

KOUROS: Look, you stand in front of me and I'll hold the reins. Hold on to the front of the chariot.

[*Laughing nervously, Psyche mimes stepping up into a chariot. She positions herself in front of him, as if standing before the driver. He holds out his arms around her, as if holding the reins, and makes clicking noises.*]

Now, are you going to tell me that my fine steeds Nyx, and Nike there, don't have being?

PSYCHE: [*Laughing in spite of herself*] No, they have being, inside your head.

KOUROS: [*Cracking the reigns and making his coconuts clop*] And aren't they responsive?

PSYCHE: [*Giggling and snuggling under his chin*] Yes, marvellously. This is fun. We could do it all afternoon.

The double doors burst open and Cupid hurries down the wide marble steps, accusation in his eyes. His wife and the boy turn, laughter still creasing their faces. For the first time, Psyche looks upon the face of her husband.

At last! There you are, dear. I wondered if we would ever see you.

Plans

Reptiles do not possess the part of the brain which evolution seems to have developed for the sole purpose of dreaming. In fact, they barely sleep at all. They just doze lightly, or fall into a kind of frozen torpor when temperatures drop and their systems fall still. In the germ of a cortex sensation bounces between forebrain, cerebellum, and medulla oblongata. There, the light is only ever bright or dim. Scent and tremor trigger a lunge or nothing at all. But there is no symbolism, no dreams of desire or denial, and no forethought. They are, in other words, happy.

Yet birds have no cerebellum but can still navigate. We, who picture with exquisite vividness our lives and our deaths, still procreate. Biology, long believed to inform desire, seems in fact to follow after it.

Sisters dream. Psyche's sisters dream and plan *diudiuque* – for a long, long, time. Then they tell her what to do.

Whet a razor, they say, and stow it just under the mattress. Light a lamp, they say, and cover the flame with a little pot. When he's lying in a stupor from your perfume and the blood-warm heat of the baby, slide out from the sheets and fetch the lamp. Take the razor, tip-toe to the bed, raise the lamp, and strike.

Men and snakes, they're all head and all tail – strike where the thick knot of muscle joins the head to the neck. We will be in the shadows, waiting for you, where we've always been.

Tyrannicide

The deaths of great things attain greater proportions than others. And behind those greater deaths is usually the desire to avenge some petty insult.

Psyche brings down the razor and the cut is already made when she recognizes her error. A hot, geyser of his blood erupts and the god bleeds out. Eros, fairest among the deathless gods, is dead.

Matter feels the loss immediately.

Far away, the sisters are seized by an incredible pain as they sit in their own homes with their husbands and servants, and they know it has been done. But there is no point in explaining, as they clutch their joints and curl in agony on the floor, because everyone else around them is doing the same. Even the house, and all the furniture and – terrifyingly – the gardens and fields, the animals in them and the sky over it all, are in the same contortions.

In the microseconds which follow (or rather, which happen all together because matter is collapsing higgeldy-piggeldy onto itself and taking space-time with it) things begin to fall apart in earnest. This is more than a general Doomsday, a Ragnarok or Frashokereti, which is unpleasant for people but leaves untouched the fabric of things. This is a returning to the universal gel of quarks and leptons, floating around in a loose gravity like an atomic cocktail party.

The strong force, Eros itself, has stopped. There is nothing now to bind quarks together to make protons, and so compose the nuclei of atoms. That magnetic power which acts upon people to pull them inexorably into each other's orbit, clashing them together to make new expressions of energy, has failed. A new, shorter-acting force of repulsion supervenes on the subatomic confusion. Every nucleus which Desire oversees bursts from the Coulomb Repulsion of the protons within it. As each nucleus pops like a Hiroshima-sized pimple, the universe groans. Only hydrogen, the survivor of the cosmos, superficially inert but full of its own inexpressible anger, remains undestroyed. Clouds of hydrogen, populated by a few odd particles

140

here and there, float in the aftermath, like old folk waiting in the rain for a bus that will never come.

There is no Cupid. There is no Psyche. Or rather, they are everywhere now, massless and drifting, reduced to evanescent sparks in the hydrogen cloud. Like the lovers they once were, their centre is everywhere and their edges nowhere. Space expands along with them and time has no meaning. At some point, the gluons and quarks that once composed them will withdraw into each other, coalescing in a familiar hot, dark, impossibly dense space from which new things will be born. What Love's role will be in this new configurations of things cannot be said. There will probably be no mouths to form words.

But this is many nanoseconds away yet. As their eyeballs collapse and disintegrate, the sisters catch sight of each other and hug themselves secretly. They have yet a few picoseconds to glory in the name of tyrannicides, Harmodius and Aristogeiton on a cosmic scale, who have liberated everything from Eros' oppression, to avenge his preference for Psyche over them.

Chimera

For some time Cupid has sensed that other things were in the bed with them.

He knows that the two conditions – the prohibition to look upon him, and the pregnancy – have recently matured within Psyche like a two-headed snake, snapping and spitting in mutual antagonism.

Does he fear that these things which moved around in the great dark bed would harm him? He could not say. He senses that his child-wife, who is swollen like an adder digesting in the sun, knows about them.

And so they pass their nights, lying breathlessly together, fearing the hidden parts of each other and longing to be out of this self-imposed labyrinth. He lies on top of the sheets and hears thunder moving closer. If it brings lightning he will turn his face away from the window. He does not want a sizzling flash and show her his face, blue as a god from the east. And lightning reminds him of family arguments in the far, but still frightening, past.

She is very close to her time now, and her fretfulness has grown with the child. She has spent much of the day miserable with anxiety, though over what he cannot say. It has something to do with her sisters' recent visit. They have filled her with discontent and a huge, nameless fear that sometimes makes her run from one end of her splendid tiny world to the other before sinking with exhaustion, keening and twisting her hands.

He knows now that their marriage was a mistake. He has asked too much of her. She is constructed of separate parts, and stress is fracturing her. The wind lashes the garden and the reeds along the river. It is drowned out by a rumble and another sound, something much closer. He sits up and calls for her in the darkness. He feels a hot, prickling dread wash over him. Something is becoming. He moans.

The thing that he has felt for weeks is in the room with them. He calls for her again. She is there – he can smell her scent in the dark, but he can also feel her unique presence.

A rumble and a crack of deafening size. In the past he has used storms to his advantage: the natural power, the convenient din, the fear so conducive to seeking comfort. Now he feels a nauseating, hot, smothering wind invading the bedroom. Something flickers; he feels seasick.

There is something close at hand, sighing and dragging itself towards the bed. The storm is rolling towards them and the house jumps as if trapped in a skipping rope turned by Typhon and Echidne.

The dragging stops and a smell like hot, half-masticated meat drifts around the bed. A footfall, like a softly-shod thing of great weight. And then it is gone, and he can feel her, his Psyche, pushing along her belly with its shipful of child filling the space.

He calls a third time, even though he knows she will not, perhaps cannot, answer. He is afraid, as he has never been afraid before.

A crack breaks directly overhead. The flash scorches the room with blue light. Deafened, almost blinded, he sees what has occupied his bed. A snake, of impossible size and monstrous, mottled scales, dragging itself through the darkness.

He screams; the lightning comes again, catching her in transition. The snake is giving way to a maned thing, leonine but with a dreadful human gaze. In the prolonged series of flashes which follows, she comes upon him through the storm that will not move from their roof. The flickering woman-snake-lion dragging itself onto the dais, through the pastos, upon the bed, and within inches of the face she was forbidden to see.

The serpent and the lion cannot laugh at the sight of the white, frightened little godlet, but the woman does as her coils crush and scoop him into her mouth, as her barbed tongue licks her mane, as the thunder roars overhead and her heart quiets at last.

The Frame

Her sisters float back to their lives, leaving Psyche with her instructions. Psyche lies on the bed on which everything has been made and feels that something is wrong. She cannot put her finger on it, but she feels as if she has just noticed some tiny movement, as you do when you lie in a covert and wait for a deer to reveal itself. This movement, she senses, is more important and more real than anything in the darkened world around her.

Abruptly, she takes a small oil lamp and the knife which has lain under the pillow for days now, and leaves the bedroom. She walks through the silent house and out into the night garden. For some reason she is surprised that it is still there. She leaves the garden, the grove, and goes into the forest. Before now, the forest has always stretched endlessly, and after a morning, an afternoon, of walking she has given up and gone back to the house. Now she walks for only a short time before the trees thin and she comes out into a cleared space and some houses touched by the moonlight.

The houses are modest; some are earthen, others have stone foundations and wooden walls. They have vegetable gardens and small enclosures for goats. The whole place smells of fires, composting matter, human life. It is a smell she has not known for – and here her memory fails her. How long has she been in her husband's house? How could all this have been so close and remained unknown to her, marooned in the pale spaces of the bedroom, the garden, the grove?

More houses appear, closer together. The soft earth is harder packed underfoot, and soon she feels a paving stone at regular intervals as the lanes become a street. She walks down the silent, built-up space and realized that the air smells different. It is a dry smell, of heat and sand and open spaces, and there is a light, insistent wind which brings something gritty and fine to her face. She passes a marketplace, four times the size of the little one in her father's town. Around the sides are stone buildings and a triumphal arch still in the process of being built. The buildings are smaller than her husband's golden palace, the stonework not as fine, but they seem more real. When she puts her hand on a wall the sandstone retains some of the day's heat.

More real, in fact, than anything she has ever known.

At a loss, she wanders around the marketplace for a while, then crosses it, rounds one of the stone buildings and sees another street, wider and finer than the others. In one house a back window stands open just above her head, covered with a grille. She wonders if it is a prison. Jumping to grab the lowest bar, she hauls herself up and catches a quick glimpse into the room, where a man sits at a table covered in papers, his head on his arms, fast asleep. An oil lamp hangs in a corner, guttering.

She goes around the side of the house. Through a gate in the wall she sees a small, fragrant garden. A fountain runs in the middle and she notices that it has the same cadence as the fountain in her husband's garden. The roses have the same perfume, the small bench catches her leg in exactly the same way. It is the same garden that she has known for many months, but smaller – and, of course, set in a town which seems always to have lain just beyond the forest. She suddenly wonders if there is another forest on the edge of this town, with another town beyond it and a garden identical to this one but smaller still, and another forest again and so on until the whole series concentrates in the centre of a single perfect rose. Her head feels strange at this, as when her tutor laid out a paradox in a childhood which blurs as she turns her memory to look at it.

At the end of the garden is a small colonnade and a door standing open to catch the night breeze. Through the door is the room she saw from the street. She enters quietly and takes in the sleeping man, whose breath stirs the papers gently. She lifts the oil lamp from its chain and relights her own, raises it just above her head and crosses on soundless feet to the table. She clutches the knife, but she knows that if the man woke and called for help she would simply give herself up.

She turns over one of the papers, which is covered in a neat hand but struck out in places where the writer has changed his mind. She reads a brief section about a girl begging to be allowed to see her sisters and a god-husband warning her that they mean her harm. Then another section, crossed out entirely, about a god whose desire to be known consumes him from the heart outwards so that he is turned partly black and ashy-fragile, and whose mother takes the guise of a beautiful girl to save him. Then other parts which have not been crossed out, of a girl jumping from a cliff into the waiting gusts of a zephyr. Of a golden house, of hot nights – described in a detail that makes her blush with recognition – and of how the desire turns to wheedling and chafing against the prohibition of seeing her divine husband's face.

Psyche reads all the scattered papers and the roaring in her ears grows as she sees her whole past, and other pasts which might have been, trapped in the pages. She sees herself, weak and silly, running in circles in this story.

The man, whom she now understands is the writer of her life, has trapped a final page under the arms that cradle his long-haired dark head. Although Psyche knows generally what is on the page – what *must* be on the page – a natural curiosity compels her to see how it ends, and to see whether she can, for once, write her own ending. Gingerly, she tugs at a corner of the page, trying to get it out without waking him.

He shifts in his sleep, a fine drool staining the page. He is young, handsome, dark-skinned. Almost as dark as a Nubian she once saw at her father's court – a Nubian, she recognizes, who was this man's idea of himself dropped into her world.

Beneath his arm she reads a line. *Tunc Psyche et corporis et animi alioquin infirma.* Then Psyche, though weak in body and spirit…

She is suddenly furious. Another scenario in which she stumbles around, weak and annoying, led on by everyone, with no more common sense than a puppy. Roughly, she jerks the page out from under his arm, spilling a drop of burning oil from the lamp onto his bare shoulder.

He sits up suddenly, crying out in pain. He sways a bit on his stool, then sees her. He sits very still. He sees that she is reading the page he had been writing when sleep overtook him.

Fati tamen saevitia sumministrante viribus roboratur, et prolata lucerna et arrepta boracula sexum audacia mutatur. … took on a manly strength because of fate's cruelty. She took out the lamp, grabbed the blade, and in her courage changed sex.

She looks at him with disgust.

'Is this the best you can do? I become manly because I *finally*,' she gestures to the pile of papers, the lives she has not led, 'get some courage up? I can't be courageous and a woman?'

He looks sheepish. 'It's just an expression.'

'Your expression is my reality.' She pushes the papers again. 'I'm so…pathetic. Things just *happen* to me, and in between times I nag and wheedle at him. You haven't even explained *why* he keeps himself hidden. Which is ridiculous, by the way.'

'I need him to be hidden for the allegory,' he says.

He cradles his shoulder, which is already showing the signs of a tight, shiny burn. Despite his pain, she wants to thump him. 'Why is *my* bad behaviour didactic and his bad behaviour's divine? It sounds like *you* need courage, not me. You could, for example, say something about gods being unreasonable.'

He looks like a man who feels things slipping away from him. 'What do you want?'

'I want to be more than you've made me,' she said. 'I want to be a hero, not just some simpering idiot. I want to go out and see the world – all the worlds. The heavens, the underworld, the world of men. I don't want to be stuck in his house with his baby and a load of voices. And I don't want a son. I'm sick of men. You limit everything. I want a daughter who will be her own woman, not just someone's wife or someone's mother. A girl who'll never need to be rescued.

147

Someone who won't be thrown off a cliff by her parents.' She looks at the table.

There is a silence except for the spitting lamp. He is ashamed of what he has put her through, this girl whom he has made a relentless seeker after the face of god, when all she wants is to be about the world. It's a fair point.

'What about your sisters?' he says.

'What about them? Do you honestly think I don't know what they're like?'

He frowns and tries to assert himself. 'I don't have to ask, you know. It's the mere stroke of my pen between you and madness. Do you want to find that it's all been a hallucination? That you're really a figment in the dream of some crone who lives in a cave?'

She looks at him coolly. 'How do you know you aren't? The very fact of me means that it's possible for the same situation to be true for you,' she gestures to the room, taking in the house, the sleeping town. 'I can crawl out from under your pen. Have you ever tried to catch the wind in a bag? That's what I could be like for you – I'll exhaust you. I'll wreck everything you create. I'll turn this paper world you've put me in upside down.'

His heart quails at the thought of it. For all the glint in her eye she sounds sad. Sad and beautiful women are, in his experience, nightmares. 'Fine,' he says. 'You'll see the world. I can turn the son into a daughter. And your sisters were redundant anyway. They've served their purpose.'

They talk quietly and with long, almost companionable pauses, until the window begins to lighten and the streets' silence is broken with cock crows, the sounds of hooves, and shouts in Punic. She gets up. Already her outline is fainter.

'Go that way.' He points to the curtain, behind which is a bed.

She turns, one hand reaching for the curtain. 'Was I ever going to see his face?'

It is the question he has dreaded, the one he has been unable to answer for the five years she has been his prisoner in the paper house of love. 'I don't know.'

She nods slowly. He wonders if she knows just how long he has been putting her through this mill.

'When I see him,' she says, 'make him beautiful. For me.'

As he draws the scroll in front of him again and picks up the pen, she raises the curtain. Behind it, now out of earshot, Psyche stands in another bedchamber, lamp in her hand and her heart in her mouth, ready to look upon the face of god.

Anagnorisis

She tightens her grip on the razor and steps towards the lamp, hidden under a pottery jar in the corner. You are what you know; your axioms are the fulcrums on which the illusion of a self turns.

Psyche stands in a small pool of lamplight, curiosity pulling her one way and piety the other. The child twists and leaps like a salmon in her belly and she cannot tell whether it is reaching for, or running from, the godhead that she is about to compromise. It seems to Psyche that this is how life really is: a state of half-darkness, half-light, longing for a sight of a god who sleeps on unaware and just out of reach.

She resolves to cross half the distance towards him and then reconsider things. She steps forward, taking her own light with her, and halts. The sleeping figure is no clearer and a black shame at the promises she will break washes over her. Thirst, shame, curiosity: it seems to Psyche that she has never felt anything but one of these three.

Desire pulls her forward; doubt halts her halfway again. The child's divinity wanes in her womb. She is exhausted by it. The only way to close this infinite gap is to take on the identity of that which is on the other side of it. The torch, she thinks, will illuminate not a man but a mirror.

Halfway forward, and halfway again, like a tortoise beneath its shell of doubt. She wonders if this is the afterlife; no Styx, no Charon or Asphodel Fields, only the infinite progression towards that which you fear and desire – which may even be yourself – held back by the Hell of your own cowardice.

The night is eternal; the increments of her crippling piety infinite. The figure on the bed never will be illuminated. Across this distance of three feet, Psyche lives her own life, and then variations of it, and then many others and their variations too and she is still an infinite number of increments away.

But finally the single flame from her lamp challenges the dark and transforms the moment. Now Psyche stands within the *kairos*, the inhuman moment when the bowstring is loaded with exactly the right force to hit the target.

Held high above his sleeping body, a single flame challenges the dark as Psyche breaks her promise and looks at him. Gradually he becomes distinct. The elements of Psyche's cosmos assemble themselves: the sandy firmament of his skin, the dark delicate line of eyelashes. The depth and measure and focus of his sleep. Psyche's heart is full.

The bedroom is a quickening crucible. The flame, recognizing its solar parent, leaps for joy. The razor turns its own edge for shame. Shadows bend over the bed to protect him. The dark is perfused with Psyche's shame. Cupid sleeps on, like a fox cub, and all the wildness lies sweetly quiet in him.

Her sisters have lied. He is not a snake. Her husband is a god. She is so disgusted with herself that she suddenly wishes she were dead. But the blade turns away from her hand and falls noiselessly to the floor, caught in the folds of her nightgown. The lamp and the man soften the hard edges of reality. He is more inward to her than he has ever been before. But now the two states – desire and disgust – are welded together.

Later, she will wonder where exactly the point of no return lay. Was it when she saw him, stretched out and massy with sleep? Or when the blade would not go into her own double-beating heart? Or when she raised the lamp higher and saw in the shadows by the bed the bow and arrows which ruin us?

Catastrophe

I am the drop of oil that burned the god.

Here is the thing about fire: it cannot lie.

Believe me, then, when I say her hand shook as she got to her feet, and her lips moved as she took in the sleeping man. I do not know what she said.

In the shadows there was a sinuous thing, a beautiful recurve bow of inlaid wood, darkened where the archer's hand had gripped it. A slim quiver of tooled leather leaned beside it, holding three black arrows with shining silver points.

Why did she touch the arrow, knowing what it was? Why did she press harder – hard enough to draw blood from her thumb? Because she was moving under a power other than will; her own nature. She was a luck-pusher, a high roller, a chancer. Out ran the blood; her luck ran out too. I felt it fleeing from her shaking hand.

She dropped the arrow back in the quiver and leaned over him. She was, I swear, incandescent – and I was her willing accomplice. They will say that I was treacherous. That I was jealous of her. That I, too, longed to pour myself over him. Do not believe it.

At last she controlled the moment, after all the nights where he controlled her.

If I had had a mouth, I would have shouted. If I had had hands, I would have clung to her.

She leaned, the lamp tipped, I fell in a shower of gold and spattered on his shoulder. A spray of oil bounced off him, struck her collarbone and scorched a matching crescent there.

I touched his shoulder; he woke, and I was between them.

He rose up like a fury and the air was full of wings, beating her back, every feather's touch scalding her. He turned angry eyes on her, gave a single flicker of disgust and regret, and he was gone.

Psyche heard the world's roar rush upon her as she was cast out into it. I wished I could have shouted something to her. *It is a great loss, what you have thrown away. But it is your loss; everyone must have one, and this is yours. At least you made it yourself.*

You ask, did it hurt to be spilled? It did not, for I was consumed by something far hotter than fire.

Ouroboros

Feeling better for the first time in months, Lucius Apuleius decides to take a walk away from the house and into the streets of Oea. He gets as far as the new triumphal arch for Marcus Aurelius before he has to sit down, his legs shaking and his heart racing from the exertion. He sits in the rhombus of shade thrown by the arch, watching the crowds come and go through it and thinks about the events that brought him there.

It occurs to him that this dizzy, weakened state was how he believed he would feel when he finally found the god. Instead it has taken a bout of the malaria he picked up in Asia to bring him to the shaking dull thrum where everything seems new, miraculous, incandescent with the life he nearly lost.

He feels long fingers of despair inch across his head like a pickpocket; it has been thirty years since his father died and he has burned up his inheritance on an education which has given him a silver tongue, a head full of philosophy, and no answers. He reviews his journey eastwards, from Madaurus to Carthage, then Athens and Rome and eventually into the vast empty spaces of Asia. There he spoke with Jews and followers of Zoroaster, Scythians who revered the horse and deer, and sitters-still who traced their origins to an Indian prince who looked into the abysm and became enlightened. Then backtracking through the ruins of Judea with its many messiahs, and Egypt's temples and temple-touts, now themselves looking to Greece for a style.

No answers anywhere. Much talk, incense, mumblings about the One and its emanations, grubby ritual couplings on Eastern altars where overpainted priests and whores parodied the emanations, and no trace of the god who had whispered to him during the blue nights of his North African childhood.

He notices that only the better-dressed actually walk through the arch. Numidians, half-Numidians like himself, and a few lighter-skinned men, attended by slaves or flunkies. The Gaetulians eye the arch and cut around it. Idly he wonders why, but his mind is addled by two months of fever, and he cannot fix on anything or draw conclusions with his accustomed rigour. He cannot even tell a decent story at dinner, which frustrates him. Only stupid, smutty stories that he picked up in taverns and hostels along his (pointless, endless) way. Horny maidservants, bungling sorcerers, cuckolded husbands, women who mate with donkeys. Ridiculous and unworthy of an education which has cost two-million sesterces.

Sitting after dinner the previous night with Sicinius Pontianus' mother Pudentilla, who sponged his fever, sent for doctors and disrupted her own peace as a widow worrying about him, he began another episode of his travels, this time about an ass who is addicted to eating roses. He felt Pudentilla watching him in the lamplight and wondered why he persisted with this stupid schoolboy's story. She heard him out to the end – the ass wins the pity of a goddess who turns him into a handsome youth, conveniently named Lucius – and she gave him a small smile.

'Is there nothing else?'

He tried to look offended. 'Nothing else? Lady, you had an ass, and roses, piety and mercy, and a handsome youth, handsomely named at the end. What else can you wish for in a story…' he tried to look pitiful, '…told by a sick man?'

She laughed at this play. 'I thought perhaps there would be more within the story. Some deeper point. It's amusing, but what do they show, all these racy tales from your travels?'

'Do they have to show anything? They make the time pass, and they make you laugh, lady.'

She came to where he sat and looked closely at him. He smelled the scent of her hair, which had only a few strands of silver, and the cream she used on her face, made of roses and argan oil. She was only a few years older than he and had been widowed for ten years. 'I can do more than laugh, Lucius. And there is more within you and your stories, which feel as if they hide something more precious than a hungry donkey.' She closed the distance between them and kisses him softly, insistently, and then is gone.

Sitting by the arch he burns with shame at the memory of it. No man likes a woman seeing through him, particularly not when she is right. He *is* insubstantial. His stories are silly, boys' jokes, and he has written nothing worth speaking of. He will return to Madaurus and become a jobbing lawyer, or worse, a teacher of rhetoric in some litter-strewn stoa, wondering where he went wrong.

He watches a couple of Italians standing in the arch, admiring the stone. Despite the heat one is in a full toga. He poses for the benefit of the other, who says something flattering. They move on. Simply framing yourself within the arch endows you with gravity, sets you off from the world around you. Lucius thinks of prayers to the One in the Mysteries. In the sand drawings he has seen in Asia, the One sits radiantly in the centre of numberless frames and each frame is the concentration of all that surrounds it. But the frames are also potentially limitless, because a reflection of the world can nest within each frame, and inside that reflection is another reflection. Endless duplication, concentration, iterations within iterations, like the stories he retells. The properties of the tale are also the properties of the universe, and the emanations of Monad to Nous, Nous to Forms, and Forms to the material world can be found in tales within tales. And they all hint at some perfect, original germ of narrative at the heart of this endless expanding matter.

But what does it all amount to? If the god lies at the heart of the tale then what is that god? How does Lucius, who is only the poor teller of this net of stories, reach it? It is worse than desire, worse than lust, this craving for communion with the eternal which has drawn him from one teacher to another, decreasing in sense and money as he went ever further east, like a man following the idea of a woman of whom he had once heard, and with which he has fallen hopelessly in love.

It is as if his whole soul is enslaved by a lover whose face he does not know.

The day has dimmed and died as he has thought these things. The well-heeled have gone home. The arch is now the temporary home of beggars, brothel-touts, children playing in the twilit streets. He watches a boy and girl playing a complicated game of blind-man's buff. The girl is poor but beautiful, a beauty she will lose to repeated childbed, but for now she is a golden-skinned thing lovelier than a goddess, her hands outstretched as the boy covers her eyes from behind. Lucius watches them for a long moment, willing her to tear the boy's hands from her eyes and to look upon his youth and strength and reward it with a kiss. The arch frames them, the girl continues blindly, laughing, and Lucius turns away.

The arch, the frame, the nest, the net. Like the ouroboros he once had tattooed beneath his left arm, eternally enclosing a sacredness by consuming its own tail. All these enclosures which hold a union, fulfilment, perhaps even love, of a kind.